"You Were…Extraordinary. As I Knew You Would Be."

His heartfelt compliment made her blush and filled her with unexpected pleasure. She shouldn't be happy that he was so impressed with her performance tonight. She should be annoyed. Sorry that she'd helped to bolster his or Ashdown Abbey's reputation in any way.

But she was pleased. Both that she'd maintained her ruse as a personal assistant, and that she'd done well enough to earn Nigel's praise.

She was candid enough with herself to admit that the last didn't have as much to do with his standing as her "boss" as with him as a man.

"Thank you," she murmured, her throat surprisingly tight and slightly raw.

"No," he replied, once again brushing the back of his hand along her cheek. "Thank you."

And then, before she realized what he was about to do, he leaned in….

Dear Reader,

Want to know a secret? I'm a huge fan of television shows like *Project Runway, Fashion Star* and *24 Hour Catwalk.* It's not the competition itself that interests me nearly as much as the creativity and construction behind the designs that eventually walk the runway.

So when my editor and I began discussing ideas for a new Harlequin Desire miniseries, *Project: Passion* leaped into my head. I just loved the idea of playing off *Project Runway* for titles, and creating characters and a world that revolves around high fashion. Plus, it seemed like the perfect excuse to watch *Project Runway* marathons and call it "research."

I can only hope you'll love the Zaccaro sisters as much as I do. Lily Zaccaro—eldest sister and founder of Zaccaro Fashions—kicks off *Project: Passion* with *Project: Runaway Heiress.* She's as protective of her business as she is of her sisters, so when someone steals her designs, her first instinct is to find out who and why. Even if her suspicions lead her straight into the arms of handsome, mouthwatering Nigel Statham, the British CEO of a rival label.

Enjoy!

Heidi Betts

HeidiBetts.com

HEIDI BETTS

PROJECT: RUNAWAY HEIRESS

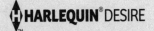

Recycling programs
for this product may
not exist in your area.

ISBN-13: 978-0-373-73238-8

PROJECT: RUNAWAY HEIRESS

Printed in U.S.A.

HEIDI BETTS

An avid romance reader since junior high, *USA TODAY* bestselling author Heidi Betts knew early on that she wanted to write these wonderful stories of love and adventure. It wasn't until her freshman year of college, however, when she spent the entire night before finals reading a romance novel instead of studying, that she decided to take the road less traveled and follow her dream.

Soon after Heidi joined Romance Writers of America, her writing began to garner attention, including placing in the esteemed Golden Heart competition three years in a row. The recipient of numerous awards and stellar reviews, Heidi's books combine believable characters with compelling plotlines, and are consistently described as "delightful," "sizzling" and "wonderfully witty."

For news, fun and information about upcoming books, be sure to visit Heidi online at HeidiBetts.com.

A huge American thank you
to U.K. reader Amanda Jane Ward, who read much of
this story and troubleshot details for me all the way to
the end to help ensure that my British hero came across
as authentic and, well, you know…British.

Any mistakes are my own—
due entirely, I'm sure, to the fact that Jason Statham
still refuses to accept my phone calls.

Thank you, Manda! If I couldn't use Jason for my
research, you were definitely the next best thing. ;)

One

Impossible. This was impossible.

Lily Zaccaro maximized her browser window, leaning in even more closely to study the photo on her laptop screen. With angry taps at the keyboard, she minimized that window and opened another.

Dammit.

Screen after screen, window after window, her blood pressure continued to climb.

More angry keystrokes set the printer kicking out each and every picture. Or as she was starting to think of them: The Evidence.

Pulling the full-color photos from the paper tray, she carried them to one of the long, wide, currently empty cutting tables and laid them out side by side, row by row.

Inside her chest, her heart was pounding as though she'd just run a seven-minute mile. Right there, before her very eyes, was proof that someone was stealing her designs.

How had this happened?

She tapped her foot in agitation, twisted the oversize dinner ring on her right middle finger, even rubbed her eyes and blinked before studying the pictures again.

The fabric choices were different, of course, as were some of the lines and cuts, making them just distinctive enough not to be carbon copies. But there was no mistaking *her* original sketches in the competing designs.

To reassure herself she wasn't imagining things or going completely crazy, Lily moved to one of the hip-high file cabinet drawers where she kept all of her records and design sketches. Old, new, implemented and scratched. Riffling through them, she found the portfolio she was looking for, dragged it out and carried it back to the table.

One after another, she drew out the sketches she'd been working on last spring. The very ones they'd been prepared to work with, manufacture and put out for the following fall's line.

After a short game of mix-and-match, she had each sketch placed beside its counterpart from her rival. The similarities made her ill, almost literally sick to her stomach.

She leaned against the edge of the table while the images swam in front of her eyes, sending a dizzying array of colors and charcoal lines into the mix of emotions that were already leaving her light-headed and nauseated.

How could this happen? she wondered again. How could this possibly have happened?

Wracking her brain, she tried to think of who else might have seen her sketches while she was working. How many people had been in and out of this studio? There couldn't have been that many.

Zoe and Juliet, of course, but she trusted them with her life. She and her sisters shared this work space. The three of them rented the entire New York apartment building, using one of the lofts as a shared living space and the other as a work space for their company, Zaccaro Fashions.

Although there were times when they got on each other's nerves or their work schedules overlapped, their partnership was actually working out surprisingly well. And Lily showed her sisters all of her design ideas, sometimes even soliciting their opinions, the same as they shared their thoughts and sketches with her.

But neither of them—not even slightly flighty party girl, Zoe—would ever steal or sell her designs or betray her in any way. Of that, she was absolutely, one hundred percent certain.

So who else could it have been? They occasionally had others over to the studio, but not very often. Most times when they had business to conduct, they did it at Zaccaro Fashions, their official, public location in Manhattan's Fashion District, where they had more sewing machines set up, with employees to produce items on a larger, faster scale; offices for each of the sisters; and a small boutique set up out front. Something they hoped to expand upon very soon.

Of course, *that* particular dream would be nearly impossible to realize if their creations continued to get stolen and put on the market before they could release them.

She collected all of the papers from the cutting table, being sure to keep each of the printed pictures with its corresponding sketch. Then she began to pace, worrying a thumbnail between her teeth and wearing out the soles of her one-of-a-kind Zoe-designed pumps while she wondered what to do next.

What *could* she do?

If she had any idea who was responsible for this, then she might know what to do. Bludgeoning them with a sharp object or having them drawn and quartered in the middle of Times Square sounded infinitely satisfying. But even going to the police would work for her, as long as the theft and replication of her clothes stopped, and the culprit was punished or fired or chased out of town by a mob of angry fashion designers wielding very sharp scissors.

Without a clue of who was behind this, though, she didn't even know where to begin. Wasn't sure she had any options at all.

Her sisters might have some suggestions, but she *so* didn't want to involve them in this.

She'd been the one to go to design school, then ask their parents for a loan to start her own business. Because—even though they were quite wealthy and had offered to simply *give* her the money, since she was already in line for a substantial inheritance—she'd wanted to do this herself, to build something rather than having it handed to her.

She'd been the one to come to New York and struggle to make a name for herself, Zoe and Juliet following along later. Zoe had been interested in the New York party scene more than anything else, and Juliet had quit her job as a moderately successful, fledgling real-estate agent back in Connecticut to join Lily's company.

Without a doubt, they had both added exponentially to Zaccaro Fashions. Lily's clothing designs were fabulous, of course, but Zoe's shoes and Juliet's handbags and accessories were what truly made the Zaccaro label a well-rounded and successful collection.

Accessories like that tended to be where the most money was made, too. Women loved to find not only a new outfit, but all the bells and whistles to go with it. The fact that they could walk into Zaccaro Fashions and walk back out with everything necessary to dress themselves up from head to toe in a single shopping bag was what had customers coming back time and time again. And recommending the store to their friends. Thank God.

But it wasn't her sisters' designs being ripped off, her sisters' stakes in the business being threatened, and she didn't want them to worry—about her or the security of their own futures.

No, she needed to handle this on her own. At least until she had a better idea of what was going on.

Returning to the laptop, she hopped up on the nearest stool and straightened her skirt, tucking her feet beneath her on one of the lower rungs. Her fingers hesitated over the keys, then she just started tapping, not sure she was doing the right thing, but deciding to follow her gut.

Two minutes later, she had the phone number of a corporate-investigation firm uptown, and five minutes after that, she had an appointment for the following week with their top investigator. She wasn't certain yet *exactly* what she would ask him to do, but once he heard her dilemma, maybe he would have some ideas.

Then she continued searching online, deciding to dig up everything she could on her newest, scheming rival, Ashdown Abbey.

The London-based clothing company had been founded more than a hundred years ago by Arthur Statham. Their fashions ranged from sportswear to business attire and had been featured in any number of magazines, from *Seventeen* to *Vogue*. They owned fifty stores worldwide, earning over ten million dollars in revenue annually.

So why in heaven's name would they need to steal ideas from her?

Zaccaro Fashions was still in its infancy, earning barely enough to cover the overhead, make monthly payments to Lily's parents toward the loan and allow Juliet, Zoe and herself to continue living comfortably in the loft and working in the adjoining studio. Ashdown Abbey might as well have been the Hope Diamond sitting beside a chunk of cubic zirconium in comparison.

The hijacked fashions in question had originated from

Ashdown Abbey's Los Angeles branch, so she dug a little deeper into that particular division. According to the company's website, it was run by Nigel Statham, CEO and direct descendant of Arthur Statham himself.

But the Los Angeles offices had only been open for a year and a half and were apparently working somewhat independently of the rest of the British company, putting out a couple of exclusive lines and holding their own runway shows geared more toward an American—and specifically Hollywood—customer base.

Which meant it wasn't all of Ashdown Abbey out to ruin Lily's life, just the Los Angeles faction.

Lily narrowed her eyes, leaning closer to the laptop screen and focusing on a photo of Nigel Statham. Public Enemy Number One.

He was a good-looking man, she'd give him that much. Grudgingly. Short, light brown hair with a bit of curl at the ends. High cheekbones and a strong jaw. Lips that were full, but not too full. And eyes that looked to be a deep shade of green, though that was difficult to tell from a picture on the internet.

She wanted to despise him on sight, but in one photo, he was smiling. A sexy, charming smile that went all the way to his eyes and threatened to turn her knees to jelly.

Of course, she was sitting and she was made of sterner stuff than that, so *that* wasn't going to happen. But at first glance, she certainly wouldn't have pegged him as a thief.

She continued to scroll through pictures and articles and company information, but much of it was for the U.K. division and the other European stores. The Los Angeles branch still seemed to be finding its footing and working to establish itself as a British clothing company on American soil.

Deciding there wasn't much more she could do until she met with the investigator except seethe in silence, Lily began to close up shop. She checked her watch. She was supposed to meet her sisters for dinner in twenty minutes, anyway.

But as she was shutting down browser windows, something caught her eye. A page filled with "job opportunities at Ashdown Abbey—U.S.A." She'd been perusing the list just to get a better idea of how the company operated.

Now, though, she expanded the window, clicked on the link for "more information" and hit Print.

It was crazy, what she was suddenly thinking. Worse yet that she was contemplating actually going through with it.

Her sisters would try to talk her out of it for sure, if she even mentioned the possibility. The investigator would undoubtedly warn her against it, then likely try to convince her to let *him* handle it at—what?—one hundred...two hundred and fifty...five hundred dollars an hour.

It would be so much easier for her to slip in and poke around herself. She knew the design world inside and out, so she would certainly fit in. And if she made herself sound smart and qualified enough, surely she would be a shoo-in.

A tiny shiver of anxiety rolled down her spine. Okay, so it was dangerous. A lot could go wrong, and she probably stood to get herself into a heap of trouble if anyone—or the *wrong* someone, at any rate—found out.

But it was too good an opportunity to pass up. Almost as though she was meant to go through with this, fate bending its bony finger to point the way. Otherwise, what were the chances *this* particular position would open up just when she most needed the inside scoop on Ashdown Abbey?

No, she had to do this. She had to find out what was going on, *how* it had happened and get it to stop. And going to work for Ashdown Abbey seemed like a good way to do exactly that.

Not just good—perfect.

Because Nigel Statham needed a personal assistant, and she was just the right woman for the job.

Two

Nigel Statham muttered an unflattering curse, slapping the company's quarterly financial report down on top of his father's latest missive. The one that made him feel like a child in short trousers being scolded for some minor transgression or another.

Handwritten on personal stationery and posted all the way from England—because that's how his parents had always done it, and email was too commonplace for their refined breeding—the letter outlined the U.S. division's disappointing returns and Nigel's failure to make it yet another jewel in the Ashdown Abbey crown since he'd been appointed CEO eighteen months ago.

Disappointment clung to the words as though his father was standing in the room, delivering them face-to-face: hands behind his back, bushy white brows drawn down in a frown of displeasure. Just like when he'd been a boy.

His parents had always expected perfection—an aim he

had fallen short of time and time again. But he hardly thought a year and a half was long enough to ascertain the success or failure of a new branch of the business in an entirely new country when it had taken nearly a century for Ashdown Abbey to reach its current level of success in the U.K. alone.

He thought perhaps his father's expectations for this new venture had been set a bit too high. But try telling the senior Statham that.

With a sigh, Nigel leaned back and wondered how long he could put off responding to the letter before his father sent a second. Or worse yet, decided to fly all the way to Los Angeles to check in on his son in person.

Another day, certainly. Especially since he was currently dreading the job of training a brand-new personal assistant.

He'd been through three so far. Three attractive but very young ladies who had been competent enough but hardly dedicated.

The problem with hiring personal assistants in the heart of Los Angeles, he decided, was that they tended to be either aspiring actresses who grew bored easily or quit as soon as they landed a part in a hand-lotion commercial; or they were aspiring fashion designers who grew bored when they didn't make it to the top with their own line in under six months.

And each time one of them moved on, he had to start all over training a new girl. It was enough to make him consider hiring an assistant to be on hand to train his next assistant.

Human resources had hired the latest in his stead, then sent him a memo with her name and a bit of background information, both personal and professional. It probably wasn't even worth remembering the woman's name, but then he'd never been *that* kind of boss.

Before he had the chance to review her résumé once more, there was a tap on his office door. Less than half a second later, it swung open and his new assistant—he deduced she was his new assistant, at any rate—strode across the carpeted floor.

She was prettier than her photo depicted. Her hair teetered somewhere between light brown and dark blond, pulled back in a loose but smoothly twisted bun at the back of her head. Her face was lightly made up, the lines classic and delicate, almost Romanesque.

A pair of dark-rimmed, oval-lensed glasses sat perched high on her nose. Small gold hoops graced her earlobes. She wore a simple white blouse tucked into the waistband of a black pencil skirt that hit midcalf, concealing three-quarters of what he suspected could prove to be extraordinary legs. And on her feet, a pair of patent-leather pumps, color-blocked in black and white with three-inch heels.

Being in fashion, he took note more than he might have otherwise. But as a man, there were certain aspects of her appearance he would have noticed regardless.

Like her alabaster skin or the way her breasts pressed against the front of her shirt. The bronze-kiss shade of her lips and rose-red tips of her perfectly manicured nails.

"Mr. Statham," she said in a voice that matched the rest of the package. "I'm Lillian, your new personal assistant. Here's your coffee and this morning's mail."

She set the steaming mug stamped with the Ashdown Abbey logo on the leather coaster on his desk. It looked as though she'd added a touch of cream, just the way he liked it.

She placed the pile of envelopes directly in front of him, and he flipped through, noticing that it seemed to be all business correspondence, no fluff to waste his time sorting out.

As first impressions went, she was making a rather positive one.

"Is there anything else I can get you?"

"No, thank you," he replied slowly.

With a nod, she turned on her heel and started back toward the door.

"Lillian." He stopped her just before she reached the doorway.

Spine straight, she returned her attention to him. "Yes, sir?"

"Are those Ashdown Abbey designs you're wearing?" he asked. "The blouse and skirt?"

She offered him a small smile. "Of course."

He considered that for a moment, almost afraid to believe that his luck in the personal-assistant department might actually be changing for the better.

Clearing his throat, he said carefully, "You wouldn't happen to be an actress, would you?" He resisted the urge to use the term *aspiring,* but only barely.

A slight frown drew her light brows together. "No, sir."

"What about modeling? Any interest in that?"

That question brought out a short chuckle. "Definitely not."

He thought back to some of the bullet points from her résumé. She hadn't simply wandered in from the street, that was for certain. Her background was in both business *and* design, with a degree in the former and a few very strong courses in the latter.

On paper she was rather ideal, but he knew as well as anyone that everybody became a bit of a fiction writer when it came to cooking up a résumé.

"And your interest in the fashion industry is…" He trailed off, leaving her to fill in the blank on her own.

For the blink of an eye, she seemed to consider what response he might be looking for. Then she replied in a firm tone, "Strictly business. And the opportunity to get my hands on fresh designs sooner than the rest of the world. I'm a bit of a clotheshorse, I'm afraid." She ended with a guileless half grin that brought out the tiniest hint of dimple in the center of her right cheek.

Almost in spite of himself, he caught his own lips turning upward. "Well, then, you've certainly come to the right place. Employees get a discount at our company store, you know."

"Yes, I know," she said slowly, and he could have sworn he saw a sparkle of devilment in her eye.

"Excellent," he murmured, feeling better about her employment already.

He hadn't exactly seen her in action, but she had, as they say, passed the first hurdle. At the very least, she hadn't walked in with a wide smile and an IQ equal to her age.

"If you haven't already, please familiarize yourself with my daily schedule and appointments for the week. There may be a few meetings and events to which I'll need you to accompany me, so watch for those notations. And be sure to review the schedule frequently, as I tend to change or update it regularly and without warning."

Picking up his coffee, he took a sip, surprised to find it quite tasty. Almost the exact ratio of cream to coffee that he preferred.

"Yes, sir. Not a problem."

"Thank you. That will be all for now," he told her.

Once again, she turned for the door. And once again, he stopped her just before she stepped out of his office.

"Oh, and, Lillian?"

"Yes, sir?" she intoned, tipping her head in his direction.

"Excellent coffee. I hope you can make an equally satisfying cup of tea."

"I'll certainly try."

With that, she closed the door behind her, leaving Nigel with a strangely unexpected smile on his face.

As soon as the door to Nigel Statham's stately, expansive office clicked shut and she was alone—blessedly, blissfully alone—Lily rushed on weak legs to the plush office chair behind her large, executive secretary's desk and dropped into it like a sack of lead.

She was shaking from head to toe, her heart both racing and pounding at the same time. It felt as though an angry gorilla was trapped inside her chest, rattling her rib cage to get out.

And her stomach…her stomach was pitching and rolling so badly, she thought she must surely know how it felt to be on a ship that was going down in a storm-tossed sea. If she *didn't* lose her quickly scarfed-down breakfast in the next ten seconds, it would be a miracle.

To keep that from happening, she leaned forward, tucking her head over her knees. Over them, because it was nearly impossible to get between them in the slim, tailored skirt she'd chosen for her first day of working undercover and with a false identity.

Lillian. *Blech.* It was the best name she'd been able to come up with that she thought she would answer to naturally, the blending of her first and middle names—Lily and Ann.

And as a last name, she'd gone with something simple and also easily identifiable, at least to her. George—what she and her sisters had called their first pet. A lazy, good-natured basset hound their father had found wandering around the parking lot where he worked.

Her mother had been furious right up until the moment she'd realized George woofed at the top of his lungs the minute anyone stepped foot on their property. From that point on, he'd been her "very best guard dog" and had gotten his own place setting of people food on the floor beside the dining-room table whenever they sat down to eat.

So Lillian George it was. Even though being referred to as Lillian made her feel like a matronly, middle-aged librarian.

Then again, she sort of looked like a librarian.

Her usual style, and definitely her own designs, leaned very strongly toward the bright, bold and carefree. She loved color and prints, anything vibrant and flirty and fun.

But for her position at Ashdown Abbey, she'd needed to be much more prim and proper. Not to mention doing as much as she could to disguise her identity and avoid being recognized or linked in any way to Zaccaro Fashions.

She could only hope that the change of name and switch to a wardrobe drawn entirely from Ashdown Abbey's own line of business attire, coupled with the glasses and darkening of her normally light blond hair would be enough to keep anyone at the company from figuring out who she really was.

It helped, too, that Zaccaro Fashions was only moderately successful. She and her sisters weren't exactly media darlings. They'd been photographed here or there, appeared in magazines or society pages upon occasion, but mostly in relation to their father and their family's monetary worth. But she would be surprised if most people—even those familiar with the industry—would recognize any one of them if they passed on the street. Although Zoe was doing her level best to change that by going out on the town and getting caught behaving badly on a more and more regular basis.

After a couple of minutes, Lily's pulse, the spinning of her head and the lurching in her stomach all began to slow. She'd made it this far. She'd made it past human resources with her creatively worded but fairly accurate résumé and her apparently not-so-rusty-after-all interview skills. Then she'd stood in front of corporate CEO Nigel Statham himself without being found out or dragged away in handcuffs.

He also hadn't followed her out of his office, shaking a finger at her deceit, or instructed security to meet her at her desk. Everything was quiet, calm, completely normal, as far as she could tell.

Ashdown Abbey certainly didn't have the hum of voices

and sewing machines in the background the way the Zaccaro Fashions offices did. But, then, Zaccaro Fashions wasn't a major, multimillion-dollar operation the way Ashdown Abbey was, either. They hadn't yet reached the point where their corporate offices and manufacturing area were two separate entities.

Frankly, Lily thought she could use the mechanical buzz of a sewing machine or her sisters' laughter as she worked with her cell phone pressed to her ear right about now. Sometimes silence was entirely overrated. Times like these, when all she could hear was her own rapid breathing and the panicked voices in her head telling her she was crazy and sure to get caught.

To keep those voices from getting any louder and leading her in the wrong direction, she started to recite one of the simple, meaningless poems she'd been forced to memorize in grade school, then slowly sat up.

Tiny stars flashed in front of her eyes, but only for a second. She blinked and they were gone, leaving her with clear vision and a clear—or clearer, anyway—head.

Nigel Statham believed she was his new personal assistant, so maybe she should go back to acting like one.

Rolling her chair up to the desk, she pulled out her computer's keyboard and mouse, and started clicking away. She'd familiarized herself with the computer's operating system just a bit before going into Nigel's office, but was sure there was much more to learn.

His daily schedule, for instance. Something she was apparently going to have to stay on top of or risk not knowing what she was supposed to be doing from one hour to the next.

She felt a small stab of guilt as she bypassed the email program, wondering if her sisters had found her note yet and honored her wishes by *not* telling anyone about her sudden disappearance or trying to track her down themselves.

She'd told them she had some personal business to attend to. Something she couldn't discuss just yet, but needed some time away to deal with. She assured them she would be fine and wasn't in any danger, and asked them to trust her to get in touch as soon as she could.

She didn't want them to worry about her, but she wasn't ready to tell them what was really going on, either. One day... one day she would fill them in on everything. She would tell them the entire story over a bottle of wine, and chances were they would have a good laugh about it.

But not until it was resolved and there was a happily-ever-after to report. When the threat to their company was gone and there were no fears or rumors left to spread like wildfire if anyone else got wind of it.

Before she left, she'd also met with Reid McCormack of McCormack Investigations about running comprehensive background checks on everyone under Zaccaro Fashions' employ. Lily honestly didn't believe he would find anything incriminating, but better safe than sorry.

And she'd informed him that she would be out of town for a while, so she would call in weekly for updates. It seemed easier than having him leave messages at the apartment, where her sisters might overhear or access them, or having him call her on her cell phone at an inconvenient moment while she was still in Los Angeles.

Frankly, she hoped he never had anything negative to report, or that if he did, it would turn out to be completely unrelated to Zaccaro Fashions—an employee with an unpaid speeding ticket or college-age drunk-and-disorderly charges that had eventually been dropped.

But until her first scheduled check-in, she needed all of her energy and brain power focused on her new job and attempts at stealth investigations.

Studying Nigel's schedule for the day, she was somewhat

relieved to see that it didn't seem to be a—quote, unquote—
heavy day for him. It looked as though he would be in his
office most of the time. He had a lunch appointment and
a conference call in the afternoon, but nothing so far that
would require her to go out with him—and hope not to be
recognized or to do something she wasn't ready or properly
trained for.

She glanced at the schedule for the rest of the week, making a mental note to check again in a couple of hours. Just
to be safe until it all became second nature to her for as long
as she was here.

She took a few minutes to investigate some of the other
programs and files on the system, but hoped she wouldn't
be expected to do too much with them too soon. Either that,
or that the company provided tutorials for the seriously lost
and computer illiterate.

What she did understand, though, was design. She knew
the vocabulary, the process and what was needed to go from
point A to point B. So she did recognize and know how to
use some of the items already installed on the PA's computer.

The question was: Could she use them to access the information she needed to track down the design thief?

Maybe yes, maybe no. It depended on whether or not Nigel
knew about the thefts.

Was he involved? she wondered.

Had he sent a mole from Ashdown Abbey into her company? Or maybe on a less despicable level, had he recognized
her designs within his company's latest collection and ignored
them? Looked the other way because it was easier and could
advance Ashdown Abbey's sales and brand recognition?

A part of her hoped not. She didn't want to think that there
were business executives out there who would stoop to such
levels just to get ahead. Not when they had a bevy of talented designers on staff already and didn't *need* to stoop to

those levels. Or that someone so handsome, with that deep, toe-curling British accent, could be capable of something so heinous. Although more attractive people had been guilty of much worse, she was sure.

It happened every day, and she wasn't naive enough to believe that just because a man was sinfully attractive and already a millionaire he wouldn't steal from someone else to make another million or two.

Not that any of her designs had earned a million dollars yet, Lily thought wryly, but the potential was there. If she could keep other companies and designers from scooping her.

Tapping a few keys, she brought up what she could find on the California Collection—the Ashdown Abbey collection that included so many of her own works, only with minor detail alterations and in entirely different textiles. Just the thought sent her blood pressure climbing all over again.

A few clicks of the mouse and the entire portfolio was on the screen in front of her, scrolling in a slow left-to-right slideshow. The flowy, lightweight summer looks were lovely. Not as beautiful as *Lily's* designs would have been, if she'd had the chance to release them, of course, but they were quite impressive.

She studied each one for as long as she could, taking in the cuts and lines. The collection mostly consisted of dresses, perfect for California's year-round sunny and warm weather. Short one-pieces, a couple of maxi dresses, and even some two-piece garments consisting of a top and skirt or a top and linen slacks.

Not all of them were drawn directly from Lily's proposed sketches. Small comfort. And it might actually work against her if she ever tried to prove larceny in a court of law.

A good defense attorney could argue that there might be *similarities* between the Ashdown Abbey and Zaccaro Fashions designs, but since the Ashdown Abbey line also included designs *without* similarities, it was obviously a mere case of creative serendipity.

Hmph.

Closing down the slideshow, Lily dug around in the other documents within the file folder. She found another graphics slideshow, this time the sketches for the final pieces that made up the California Collection.

They were full color and digital, done on one of the many art and design computer programs that were becoming more and more popular. Even Lily had one of them on her tablet, but she still preferred pencil and paper, charcoal and a sketch pad, and actual fabric swatches pinned to her hand-drawn designs over filling in small squares of space with predetermined colors or material samples on a digitized screen.

But what caught her attention with these designs wasn't *how* they were done, it was the fact that they were signed. Ashdown Abbey apparently had design teams on the payroll rather than one designer in charge of his or her own collection.

Moving from the graphics files to the text files, she found a list of the California Collection's entire design team, complete with job titles and past projects they'd worked on for Ashdown Abbey. A jolt of adrenaline zipped through her, and she hurried to send the list to the printer.

The zip-zip of the machine filled the quiet of the cavernous outer office. It rang all the louder in her ears for the fact that she didn't want to get caught.

When a buzz interrupted the sound of the printer, Lily jumped. Then she looked around, searching for the source of the noise. Finally, she realized it was coming from the phone, one of the lights on the multiline panel blinking in time with the call of the intercom.

Chest tight, she took a deep breath and pressed the button for Nigel Statham's direct line.

"Yes, sir?" she answered.

"Could I see you for a moment?"

The abrupt request was followed by total silence, and she realized he'd hung up without waiting for a reply.

Grabbing the list of designers from the printer tray, she folded it over and over into a small square and stuffed it into the front pocket of her skirt. Patting the spot to make sure it was well concealed, she strode to the door of Nigel's office, unsure of what she would encounter on the other side. She didn't even know if she should bring a pad and pencil with her to take notes.

What did personal assistants automatically pick up when summoned by the boss? Paper and pen? A more modern electronic tablet? She hadn't even had a chance to poke around and find out what was provided for Nigel Statham's executive secretary.

So she walked in empty-handed after giving one quick tap on the door to announce her arrival.

Nigel turned from typing something into his own computer to jot a note on the papers in front of him before lifting his attention to Lily. She stood just behind one of the guest chairs, awaiting his every request.

"What are you doing for dinner this evening?" he asked.

The question was so far from anything she might have expected him to say, her mind went blank. She was quite sure her face did, too.

"I'll take that to mean you don't have plans," he remarked.

When she still didn't respond, he continued, "I'm having dinner with a potential designer and thought you might like to join us. Having you there will help to keep things on a business track, as well as better familiarize you with your position."

For lack of anything more inspired to say, she replied with a simple, "All right."

Nigel gave an almost imperceptible nod. "I'll be leaving

from the office, but you're welcome to go home and change, or take a bit of a rest, if you like. I'll come round for you at eight. Be sure to leave your address before you finish for the day."

He returned his attention to his work, giving Lily the impression that plans for the evening had been decided and she'd been dismissed.

"Yes, sir," she said, because she thought it was respectful and some sort of acquiescence was needed. Then she tacked on a short "Thank you" for good measure before hurrying back out to the reception area.

Taking a seat behind her desk, she tried to decide how she felt about this latest turn of events.

On the one hand, she already had a list of designers for the Ashdown Abbey collection based on her work. She considered that quite a coup for her first day in the enemy's camp.

On the other, her most fervent prayer had been merely to get through the day without being found out. She'd never imagined she would be asked to put in extra time outside the office. Especially not *alone* with the boss.

Of course, she wouldn't really be *alone* with him. It was a business dinner, so at least one other person would be there. But it was still an after-hours situation in much-too-close proximity to the man who held her future in his hands.

Her professional future and possibly her very freedom.

Because if he ever learned who she really was and why she was working incognito within his company, she'd likely find herself behind bars. No amount of crying "he was mean to me first" would save her then.

Three

At five minutes to eight, Lily was still racing around her apartment, trying to be ready before Nigel arrived.

It didn't help that she'd just moved in and had brought very little with her from New York. Or that this was supposed to be merely a place to sleep. Nothing fancy. Nothing expensive—at least by Los Angeles standards. Simply somewhere to rest and hunker down with her suspicions and evidence while she worked days at Ashdown Abbey.

Never had she imagined that her boss—CEO of the entire company—would decide to "drop by" and pick her up for dinner.

And then there was the fact that she hadn't planned for after-hours job requirements. Once she'd arrived, she'd filled her closet with Ashdown Abbey business attire, not only to fit in, but to subconsciously give Nigel Statham and everyone else the impression that she absolutely belonged there. But she hadn't purchased a single item for an evening out.

Granted, she could probably get away with wearing the same skirt and blouse that she'd worn that day. If she was attending this meal as Nigel's personal assistant, then it couldn't hurt for her to look like one.

But she suspected Nigel's choice of restaurant might be of the highly upscale variety, and she didn't want to stand out. Or worse, blend in with the servers.

So she'd done the best she could with what her limited current wardrobe had to offer.

Another black skirt, shorter this time, with a sexy—but not too sexy—slit up the back. A sheer, nearly diaphanous sapphire-blue blouse that she'd intended to wear as a shell over a more modest chemise top. Now, though, she wore it over only a bra.

She'd checked and double-checked in the mirror to be sure the effect wasn't trashy. Thankfully, the bra was barely visible, even though in certain light, flashes of skin could be seen beneath the top.

To dazzle it up even more, she added sparkling chandelier earrings, a matching *Y* necklace, and open-toed four-inch heels that—now that she was wearing them—might be a bit too suggestive for nine-to-five. They were more than appropriate for a night out on the town, though, professional or otherwise.

She threw a few items like her wallet, a lipstick, keys and her cell phone—just in case—in a small, plain-black clutch, and *finally* thought she was ready enough to jump when Nigel arrived.

She'd just taken a deep, stabilizing breath and was contemplating one last visit to the restroom when the doorbell rang.

Whatever calm she'd managed to find with that long inhalation evaporated at the shrill, mechanical sound, and a lump of dread began to grow in the pit of her stomach.

Fingers curled around her purse, she swallowed hard and

moved to the door. Because she didn't want Nigel peeking inside and seeing that there were no personal touches to the apartment to affirm her claims of having lived in the city for several years, she opened it only a crack, using her body to block his view.

As quickly and smoothly as she could, she slipped out into the hallway, pulling the door closed and locked behind her. Leaning back, she used the doorjamb to prop herself up, feeling suddenly overwhelmed and overly scrutinized.

Nigel's hazel eyes studied her from head to toe. He was standing so close, she could see the specks of green dotting his irises and smell his spicy-with-a-hint-of-citrus cologne.

She inhaled, drawing the scent deeper into her lungs, then realized what she was doing and stopped, holding her breath in hopes that he wouldn't notice her small indiscretion.

It was not a good idea to start thinking her boss smelled good. She already found him attractive, simply because he was. Anyone, female or male, would have to agree based on his physical attributes alone. Much the way everyone knew the sky was blue, a handsome man was a handsome man.

That didn't mean she should be building on that initial assessment by adding "smells really good" to the tally.

He was a good-looking man with exceptional taste in cologne, that's all. Lily hoped that others might consider her on the pretty side with good taste in perfume, as well. Especially after how much time she'd put into her appearance tonight.

Nigel—her boss, her attractive and well-scented *boss*—returned his gaze to her face.

"You look lovely," he commented. "Ready to go?"

"Yes."

To her surprise, he offered his arm. There was nothing romantic in the gesture, only politeness. After a short hesitation, she slipped her hand around his elbow and let him lead her down the well-lit, utilitarian hallway of the apartment building.

Would an American man have acted so gentlemanly, or was it just Nigel's British upbringing? Whatever the case, she liked it. Maybe a little too much.

They walked down the three short flights of stairs rather than waiting for the elevator. Outside, the early evening air was fresh and cool, but not cold. A long, silver Bentley Mulsanne waited at the curb, and Nigel opened the rear door, holding it while she got in.

She'd intended to slide across so he could climb in behind her, but there was a rather large console turned down between the two rear seats, as well as fold-out trays on the back of the front seats. The one on his side was down, with an open laptop resting on it.

While she was still marveling at the awesome interior of the luxury vehicle, Nigel opened the door opposite hers and took his place, quickly closing the computer and tray.

"Sorry about that," he said, moving the laptop out of the way on the floor beside his briefcase.

When she didn't respond—she was apparently sitting there frozen, like a raccoon caught rummaging through household garbage—he returned the center console to its upright position, then leaned past her to pluck the seat belt, stretch it across her motionless form and click it into place.

As he stretched to reach, his arm brushed her waist, terribly close to the underside of her breasts. A shiver of something very un-employee-like skated through her, warming places that had no business growing warm. She swallowed and tried to remain very still until the sensation passed.

Nigel, of course, had no idea of the response he'd caused by such an innocent action. And with luck, he never would.

Licking her lips, she tamped down on whatever was rolling around under her skin and made sure her lips were turned up in at least an imitation of a smile.

"Thank you," she said, tugging at the safety belt to show that she was, indeed, alive and well and capable of simple human functions. "It looks like you're working overtime," she added, relieved that her voice continued to sound steady and normal.

He leaned back in the seat, running his hands along his thighs and letting out a breath as he relaxed a fraction. "There doesn't seem to be overtime with this position. It's round-the-clock."

Lily certainly knew what he meant by that. She'd worked twenty-four/seven to establish the Zaccaro label. Then when her sisters had joined in, the three of them had given all they had to get the company truly up and running.

Even now that they had their boutique open and were producing items on more than a one-off basis, life was no less stressful or busy. They'd simply exchanged one set of problems for another. And having an office-slash-studio at home only kept the work closer at hand.

"For tonight's dinner," Nigel began in that accent that would be charming even if the looks and personality didn't match—at least to her unaccustomed American ears, "we're meeting with a designer who's looking to move from Vincenze to a higher position at Ashdown Abbey."

Lily's eyes widened a second before she schooled her expression. Vincenze was a huge, multimillion-dollar design enterprise. A household name and very big deal. If she wasn't busy running her own fashion-design business, she would have been ecstatic over the possibility of going to work for them.

Yet tonight they were meeting with someone who wanted to *leave* Vincenze for Ashdown Abbey.

Which wasn't to say Ashdown Abbey was a lesser label.

Far from it. If anything, Ashdown Abbey and Vincenze were similar when it came to levels of success. But their design aesthetics were entirely different, and it would definitely take some doing—at least in her experience—for a designer to go from one to the other without traversing a sharp learning curve.

Fighting to keep her mind on the job she was *supposed* to be doing rather than the one that came more naturally to her, Lily said, "I'm not sure exactly what my role is this evening."

"Just listen," he replied casually. "It will be a good way for you to learn the ropes, so to speak."

He turned a little more in her direction and offered a warm smile. "Frankly, I asked you to join me so I wouldn't have to be alone with this fellow. These so-called business dinners can sometimes drone on, especially if the potential employee attempts to regale me with a long list of his or her talents and abilities."

Lily returned his grin. She knew what he meant; the fashion industry was filled with big mouths and bigger egos. She liked to think she wasn't one of them, but there was a certain amount of self-aggrandizing required to promote oneself and one's line.

"Maybe we should work out a signal and some prearranged topics of discussion," she offered. "That way if things get out of hand and your eyes begin to glaze over, you can give me a sign and I'll launch into a speech about global warming or some such."

Nigel's smile widened, showing a row of straight, sparkling-white teeth. "Global warming?" he asked, the amusement evident in his tone.

"It's a very important issue," she said, adopting a prim-and-proper expression. "I'm sure I could fill a good hour or two on the subject, if necessary."

He nodded a few times, very slowly and thoughtfully, his

lips twitching with suppressed humor. "That could certainly prove useful."

"I thought so," she agreed.

"What would you suggest we use as a signal?"

She thought about it for a minute. "You could tug at your earlobe," she said. "Or kick me under the table. Or perhaps we could have a code word."

"A code word," he repeated, one brow lifting with interest. "This is all starting to sound very…double-oh-seven-ish."

Appropriate, she supposed, since he reminded her a little of James Bond. It was the accent, she was sure. Her stomach tightened briefly.

Feigning a nonchalant attitude she didn't entirely feel, she shrugged. "Spies are good at what they do for a reason. But if you'd prefer to be trapped for hours by a potential employee you can't get away from, be my guest."

Silence filled the rear of the car, only the sound of the tires rotating beneath them audible as the seconds ticked by and Lily's anxiety grew.

She might have overstepped her bounds. After all, she'd only been in this man's employ for twelve hours. That might have been a bit too early to start voicing her opinions and telling him what to do.

Worse, she probably shouldn't have jumped on his mention of James Bond movies and followed the spy thread. Because technically, *she* was a spy within his organization, and she didn't want him spending too much time wondering how she knew so much about the business of espionage.

"I definitely agree that an escape plan is in order," Nigel said, finally breaking the nerve-inducing quiet. "How would it be if I inquired about your headache from earlier? You can say that it's come back and you'd really like to get home so you can rest."

"All right." It sounded as good as anything else they might

come up with, and she certainly knew more about headaches than she did about global warming.

"And if *you* grow bored," he continued, "you can ask me if I'd like another martini. I'll decline and say that we should get going, as I have an early appointment in the morning, anyway."

"Will you be drinking martinis?" she asked.

"Tonight, I will," he said, a spark of mischief lighting his eyes. "It will bolster our story, if we make an excuse to leave the restaurant early."

"We haven't even arrived at dinner yet, and already we're thinking of ways to get away as soon as we've finished eating," she remarked.

"That's because it's a boring, uptight business dinner. If this were a dinner date, I would already be considering options for drawing things out. Excuses to keep you there well past dessert."

Lily's heart skipped a beat, her palms growing damp even as a wave of unexpected heat washed over her. That was not the sort of thing she expected to hear from her boss. It didn't *feel* like a benign, employer-to-employee comment, either. It felt much too…suggestive.

And on top of that, she was suddenly picturing it: a dinner date with Nigel rather than a business dinner. Sitting across from him at a candlelit table for two. Leaning into each other as they spoke in soft tones. Flirting, teasing, building toward something much more serious and intimate.

The warmth grew, spreading through her body like a fever. And when she imagined him reaching out, touching her hand where it rested on the pristine white linen of the tablecloth, she nearly jumped, it seemed so real.

Thankfully, Nigel didn't notice because the car was slowing, and he was busy readjusting his tie and cuff links.

Lily licked her lips and smoothed her hands over her own

blouse and skirt, making sure she was as well put together as he was.

When the car came to a complete stop, he looked at her again and offered an encouraging half smile. "Ready?" he asked.

She nodded just as Nigel's door was opened from the outside. He stepped out, then turned and reached back for her.

Purse in hand, she slid across the wide seat and let Nigel take her arm as she stepped out. His driver nodded politely before closing the door and moving back around the hood of the car to the driver's seat.

Looking around, Lily realized they were standing outside of Trattoria. She wasn't from Los Angeles, but even she recognized the name of the elegant five-star restaurant. To her knowledge, the waiting list for reservations was three to four months long.

Unless, she supposed, you were someone like Nigel. The Statham name—and bank account—carried a lot of weight. Not only in L.A. or England, either, but likely anywhere in the world.

She was no stranger to fine dining, of course. She'd grown up at country clubs and taken international vacations with her parents. She even knew a few world-renowned master chefs and restaurateurs personally.

But she wasn't with her family now, and hadn't lived that way for several years; she'd been too busy working her fingers to the bone and building her own company the old-fashioned way.

She was also supposed to be from more of a blue-collar upbringing, not a secret, runaway heiress. Which meant she shouldn't be familiar with seven-course meals, real silverware or places like this, where appetizers started at fifty dollars a plate.

The good news was that she wouldn't embarrass herself

by not knowing which fork to use. The bad news was that she needed to act awed and out of her element enough not to draw suspicion. From anyone, but especially Nigel.

Passing beneath the dark green awning lined with sparkling lights, he led her past potted topiaries and through the wide French doors at the restaurant's entrance.

A tuxedoed maître d' met them immediately, and as soon as Nigel gave his name, they were led across the main dining area, weaving around tables filled with other well-dressed customers who were talking and laughing and seemed to be thoroughly enjoying their expensive meals.

At the rear of the restaurant, the maître d' paused, waving to a medium-size table set for four where another man was already seated.

Rounding the table, Nigel held a chair out for her while the other man rose. He was young—mid to late twenties, Lily would guess—with dark hair and an expensive suit. Most likely a Vincenze, even one of his own designs, since that's where he was currently working.

"Mr. Statham," the designer greeted Nigel, holding out his hand.

Nigel waited until she was seated to reach across the table and shake.

"Thank you for meeting with me."

Nigel inclined his head and introduced them. "Lillian, this is Harrison Klein. Mr. Klein, this is my assistant, Lillian George."

"Pleased to meet you," Harrison said, taking her hand next.

When they were all seated, a waiter brought leather-bound menus and took their drink orders. True to his word, Nigel ordered a dry martini. He even made a point of asking for it "shaken, not stirred," then turned to her with a humorous and entirely too distracting wink.

Soon after they placed the rest of their orders, their salads

nd entrées arrived, and they made general small talk while
hey ate. Nigel asked questions about Klein's schooling and
experience and his time at Vincenze.

It was odd to be sitting at a table with another designer and
he CEO of one of the biggest labels in the United Kingdom—
nd soon possibly the United States—without adding to the
discussion. So many times, she had to bite her tongue to keep
from asking questions of her own or inserting her two cents
ere and there into the conversation.

In order to avoid saying something she shouldn't, she
stayed busy sipping her wine, toying with the stem of her
glass, studying the lines of each of their outfits. Mentally she
deconstructed them, laying out patterns, cutting material and
sewing them back up.

Finally, they were finished with their meals and the table
was cleared. Nigel declined the dessert menu for all of them,
but asked for coffee.

And then he held out a hand to the other man. "Your portfolio?"

Harrison's Adam's apple bobbed as he swallowed nervously, but he leaned over and retrieved his portfolio from
the floor beside his chair. He passed it to Nigel, then sat back
and waited quietly.

Lily found her pulse kicking up just a fraction. This was
such an important, nerve-racking moment for any designer.
She still wondered why someone who already had a job at a
successful design corporation would be interested in moving.

She had gone an entirely different route, striking out on
her own to establish a personal label and company instead
of taking a job elsewhere and working her way up the ladder.

In a lot of ways, that would have been easier. It might have
taken her longer to form her own label and have her own
storefront, but she certainly would have learned from the
best and maybe avoided some of the pitfalls she'd encoun-

tered while barreling ahead with her one-woman—and then three-woman, thank goodness—show.

The tension at the table thickened as Nigel studied the portfolio carefully, page by page. Sitting beside him, Lily could see each design clearly, and couldn't resist drinking them in.

After several long minutes, Nigel closed the portfolio and passed it back. "Very nice, Harrison, thank you."

From the other man's expression, Lily could tell he'd been hoping for a far more exuberant response. She almost felt sorry for him.

"We'd best call it an evening," Nigel continued, "but we have your résumé and contact information, and will be in touch."

Klein's face fell, but he recovered quickly. "I appreciate that. Thank you very much," he said, holding out his hand.

The two men shook, putting a clear end to the dinner meeting. But Lily couldn't resist tossing in a quick, "Are you sure you wouldn't like another martini?"

Nigel raised a brow in her direction, one corner of his mouth twitching in mirth.

"No, thank you. I've had quite enough to drink. I think it would be best if we call it a night, especially considering our early morning meetings."

Biting back her personal amusement, she nodded. The three of them rose, said their goodbyes and headed out of the restaurant. It took a few minutes for Nigel's car to arrive, but they were silent until they were closed inside and the vehicle was slowly moving again.

"So," Nigel began, shifting on the wide leather seat to face her more fully. "What did you think?"

Somewhat startled by the question, Lily swallowed. "About what?"

"Klein," he intoned. "The interview. His designs."

What a loaded set of questions, she thought. She had opinions, to be sure. But as his personal assistant, should she be spouting them off? And what if she said too much, revealed herself as being too knowledgeable for such a low-level position?

"It's all right. You can speak freely," he said, almost as though he'd read her mind. "I want your honest opinion. It doesn't mean I'll listen, but I'm curious all the same. And it won't have an impact on your position at Ashdown Abbey one way or the other, I promise."

Hoping he was as good as his word, she gave a gentle shrug. "He's talented, that's for certain."

"But…"

"No buts," she corrected quickly. "He's clearly very talented."

Nigel kept his gaze locked on her, laser eyes drilling into her like those of a practiced interrogator.

"Fine," she breathed on a soft sigh. "He's very talented, *but*…I don't think his designs are at all suitable for Ashdown Abbey."

"Why not?" he asked in a low voice.

"Ashdown Abbey is known for its high-end business attire, even though you've recently branched out into casual and sportswear. But Klein's aesthetic leans more toward urban hip. I can see why he's done well at Vincenze—they've got a strong market in New York and Los Angeles with urban street and activewear. But Ashdown Abbey is a British company, known for clothes that are a bit more professional and clean-cut."

She paused for a moment, wondering if she'd said too much or maybe overstepped her bounds.

"Unless you're planning to move in that direction," she added, just to be safe.

Long seconds ticked by while Nigel simply stared at her,

not a single thought readable on his face. Then one side of his mouth lifted, the hazel-green of his eyes growing brighter.

"No, we have no plans to move in that direction for the time being," he agreed. "Your assessment is spot-on, you know. Exactly what I was thinking while I flipped through his designs."

For a moment, Lily sat in stunned silence, both surprised and delighted by his reaction. She so easily could have screwed up.

With a long mental sigh of relief, she reminded herself that she was supposed to be poised and self-assured. She'd lobbied for the job as his PA by making it clear she knew her stuff. As long as she didn't let anything slip about her true identity or reason for being there, why shouldn't she let a little of her background show?

"Maybe you'll be glad you hired me, after all," she quipped.

He gave her a look. A sharp, penetrating look that nearly made her shrink back inside her shell of insecurity.

And then he spoke, his deep voice and spine-tingling accent almost making her melt into the seams of the supple leather seat.

"I think I already am."

Four

Though she insisted it wasn't necessary, Nigel walked Lillian to the front door of her flat. It was the least he could do after eating up her evening with Ashdown Abbey business.

He hadn't actually needed her to accompany him to the restaurant this evening. Past personal assistants had certainly attended business functions such as that, but most had taken place during normal working hours. He'd never before requested that his assistant go to dinner with him—even a business dinner.

He wasn't entirely sure why he'd made the request of Lillian. Perhaps he'd hoped to test her mettle because she was so new on the job. They'd had a mere handful of hours together at the office, during which she'd impressed him very much. But he'd wanted to see her outside of the office, in a more critical corporate situation, to see how she handled herself in the real world, when faced with real Ashdown Abbey business associates.

But that was only what he was telling himself. Or what he'd tell others, should he be asked.

The truth lay somewhere closer to him simply not being ready to say goodbye to her company just yet.

She was quite attractive. Something he probably shouldn't have noticed…but then, he was human and male, and it was rather difficult to miss.

The package she put together intrigued him, and he'd decided to find a way to study her a bit more closely and for a while longer.

Coercing her into going to dinner with him might not have been the wisest decision he'd ever made as an employer toward an employee, but it had been quite enlightening.

Lillian George, it turned out, was not only beautiful but smart, as well. In the car, she'd been witty and charming. Though she'd started out nervous—at least by his impression—she'd quickly loosened up and even begun to tease him with her notion of creating a plan for their escape from a boring dinner meeting.

Then, at dinner itself, she'd been nearly the perfect companion. Quiet and unassuming, yet brilliant at making small talk and knowing when to speak and when to remain silent. Definitely an excellent performance from his personal assistant.

Not for the first time, though, he wondered what she might be like over a dinner that had nothing to do with business.

His mind shouldn't be wandering in that direction, he knew, but once the thought filled his head, he couldn't seem to be rid of it. It would have been nice to focus his full attention on her throughout the meal, and to feel the same from her. To talk about something other than Ashdown Abbey and potential new designs or designers, and to chat about the personal instead of business.

How long had it been since he'd taken a woman to dinner or out on the town?

Not since Caroline, for certain.

And a beautiful woman who had nothing to do with his family's company...?

Well, Caroline definitely didn't qualify there. She hadn't been involved with Ashdown Abbey when they'd first met, but she *had* been an American model eager to sleep her way to the lead in their runway shows and ad campaigns—preferably in the U.K. so that she could go "international."

And the random models he was often seen with at fashion-industry functions simply didn't count.

But then, neither did tonight. Not really. Though a part of him wished it could.

They made their way down the narrow hall of her building, coming to a stop in front of the door to her flat. She fit her key into the lock and turned it, but didn't open the door. Instead, she turned back round to face him, the knob still in her hand, one arm twisted behind her.

"Thank you," she said softly. "I had a very nice time tonight."

"Even though I forced you to come along as part of your role as my assistant?" he couldn't help but inquire.

She smiled gently at him. "Even though. I appreciated the chance to sit in on one of your meetings. I know how important something like that is. And I appreciate that you let me voice my opinion on Harrison Klein's work. You certainly didn't have to ask when I've only been working for you a single day."

"That's *why* I asked," he told her. "I wanted to know what you were made of, and that seemed a fast way to find out."

"So I passed your little test?" she asked, tipping her head slightly to one side.

"With flying colors," he said without hesitation.

"I guess that means I still have a job and should go ahead and show up in the morning."

"Most definitely. Keep up the good work, and I may just promote you to VP of the company."

"I'm sure the current vice president would be delighted to hear that."

Nigel shrugged. "Eh. It's my uncle. But he's a grumpy old sod and should probably be retiring soon, anyway."

Lillian laughed, the sound light with only a hint of nerves.

Were they the nerves of an executive secretary having a frank discussion with her new boss? Or of a woman standing much too close to a man in an empty hallway?

Knowing he was skating dangerously near the line that separated personal from professional, Nigel straightened and cleared his throat.

"Well," he murmured. "I should let you go inside and get to bed, since I know you have to be at work early tomorrow. Thank you again for your company this evening."

"Thank you for a delicious meal. It was a treat to be able to sit at Trattoria and order more than tap water with a slice of lemon."

He chuckled at that. It hadn't occurred to him that his restaurant of choice might be that far out of the realm of normalcy for Lillian. But now that he thought about it, Trattoria was almost certainly too pricey for an assistant's salary. Even an executive assistant's.

"I'm glad you enjoyed it. Good night, then."

Placing his hands on her upper arms, he leaned in and pressed a quick kiss to her cheek. Quick and entirely innocent…but one he found himself wishing could be longer and much *less* innocent.

Juliet Zaccaro paced the length of the living room in the loft apartment she shared with her two sisters.

"I don't know what you're so worried about," her youngest sister, Zoe, said from where she sat in the corner of the sofa.

She was curled up, nonchalant and bored. More concerned with her latest manicure than their middle sister's well-being.

"How can you say that?" Juliet all but snapped. "Lily has been missing for a week."

"She left a note," Zoe returned. "She told us not to worry about her, and not to look for her. Obviously, she knows what she's doing and needs some time away."

Zoe might have been speaking the truth, but that didn't mean Juliet had to like it. Or agree.

"I don't care," she said, crossing her arms beneath her breasts and pausing in her pacing to tap her foot angrily. "This isn't like her. What if something is wrong?"

"If something was wrong, Lily would tell us," was Zoe's bored and yet utterly confident reply. "She's never exactly been shy about asking for help before."

Juliet's brows pulled together in a frown. She really hated it when Zoe—the youngest, flightiest, most self-absorbed of the Zaccaro sisters—was also the sensible one.

"Well, it can't hurt to look for her. *Ask* her face-to-face if everything is okay."

Absently, she twisted the gold-and-diamond engagement ring on her left ring finger around and around. Where in heaven's name could Lily have gone? *Why* would she run off like this? It wasn't in her sister's nature at all to disappear without a word…or to disappear after leaving only a brief, cryptic note.

Juliet might have been the oldest of the Zaccaro girls and stereotypically the responsible one, taking her role as big sister seriously, but Lily was no empty-headed blonde slacker. She'd started her own fashion line that had evolved into her own company. She'd been successful enough and dogged enough to bring Juliet and Zoe in as partners to help her run the company with her.

These were not the actions of someone who would wake up one morning and decide she wanted to be a beachcomber instead. Not when there was so much going on at Zaccaro Fashions right now, so many balls in the air that Lily was juggling almost single-handedly.

Juliet and Zoe helped where they could, but…well, Zoe tended to be easily distracted, and they never knew if she would show up clearheaded and raring to go or call from Las Vegas to say she'd met a guy and would be back in a couple of weeks.

And Juliet was nearly ready to yank her hair out. In addition to overseeing handbag and accessory design for Zaccaro Fashions, she had her wedding to plan. And her moody, sometimes demanding fiancé to keep happy… She hadn't told her sister yet, but Paul had begun pressuring her—strongly—to move back to Connecticut after their honeymoon. He'd seemed fine with her life in New York when he'd proposed. She'd been here more than a year already, and he'd acted as though he was supportive of her new career direction and would be more than willing to move down to be closer to her.

Then she'd said yes, accepted his proposal and things had slowly started to change. It bothered her. Concerned her, even. But the date had been set, the venue reserved, a caterer hired, flowers chosen… How could she back out now just because her feet were getting a little chilly?

As she kept telling herself, multiple times a day, it would pass. Dragging her thoughts back to the matter at hand, she stalked across the hardwood floor to the kitchen island and slid open the drawer where they kept everyday odds and ends. Pencils and pens, paper clips, a pair of scissors and the thick borough of Manhattan phone directory.

She pulled it out and flipped to the yellow, paid-advertisement section, looking for listings for private detectives or investigators or whatever they were called. Maybe one of them could figure out what had happened to Lily, because she was sure staggering around in the dark. She had no idea where to begin looking for her sister, or even who to call to ask about her possible whereabouts.

As she got closer to the *P*s, the directory fell open, and she noticed a stiff business card stuck between the tissue-thin pages. Plucking it out, she turned it over and read the black print on a plain white background.

McCormack Investigations
Corporate. Private.

She had no idea where the card had come from, but judging by the corresponding ad on the page in front of her, it was probably one of the numbers she'd have called, anyway.

Taking the card with her, she marched back across the living room, casting an annoyed glance at Zoe, whose attention had been drawn to the latest issue of *Elle*.

"I'll be in my room," Juliet muttered through her teeth.

Tipping her head over the back of the sofa, Zoe watched her go. With an exaggerated sigh, she closed the magazine and tossed it on the coffee table.

"Okay. I think I'll go over to the studio to work for a while. Let me know if you want to go out for dinner."

Even if they made plans, chances were Zoe would change her mind and zip off to some club at the last minute, leaving Juliet to her own devices.

She waited until Zoe was gone and she was alone to pull out her cell phone and dial the number for McCormack Investigations. It took her a few minutes to convince the receptionist that her problem was a serious one and that time was of the essence, though she didn't go into a lot of detail.

The woman collected her name and contact information, promising to pass her message along and get back to her as soon as possible.

Juliet would have preferred being put on the phone with one of the company's investigators immediately or being told she could come in first thing in the morning to meet with someone in person. But she knew her dilemma wasn't exactly an emergency—at least not yet.

And please, God, don't let it become one. The idea of something happening to her sister made Juliet's blood run cold.

So she agreed to stay by the phone and told herself not to panic, not to let her imagination race out of control.

She should go over to the studio with Zoe and try to get some work done. Keep her mind off Lily and the phone in her hand that refused to ring, even after five whole minutes of waiting.

Instead, she resumed pacing a path through the middle of the living-room area. Which was much easier without Zoe in the way, distracting her with her sensible arguments and assurances that Lily was just fine.

Step. Step. Step.

Tick. Tick. Tick.

Turn.

Step. Step. Step.

Tick. Tick. Tick.

Five minutes turned into ten. Ten into twenty.

She stopped. Worried her thumbnail. Tapped her foot. Went back to pacing.

At thirty minutes and counting, she let out a huff of breath and dropped into the center of the sofa, the cushion wheezing at the sudden addition of her weight.

When her cell phone pealed, she jumped and let out a startled yip. She'd been concentrating so hard on making the stupid thing ring that when it finally did, it scared the bejesus out of her.

Heart pounding for more reasons than one, she brought it to her ear and whispered, "Hello?"

"Ms. Zaccaro?"

"Yes."

"This is Reid McCormack from McCormack Investigations. I have here that your sister is missing and you'd like help tracking her down."

"Yes," she said again.

"You understand, don't you, that she's an adult and is allowed to leave town without telling anyone where she's going," the man on the other end of the line intoned.

Through gritted teeth, Juliet responded, "Yes."

"And if she left a note…she did leave a note, correct?"

Hoping she didn't end up with a cracked molar after this conversation, she ground out yet another, "Yes."

"If she left a note, then she really can't be considered missing. The police would tell you to wait and hope you hear from her. And that you can't file a missing-persons report unless there are actual signs of foul play."

Feeling deflated and more frustrated than ever, Juliet dropped her head and murmured a dejected, "I understand."

A beat passed before Reid McCormack spoke again.

"So why don't you come by tomorrow around 11:00 a.m.? I can't promise anything. I may not even be able to look for your sister. But we'll talk. All right?"

His low-timbred, slowly spoken words had Juliet's head shooting up so fast, it left her dizzy.

Had she heard him correctly? Clearing her throat, she swallowed and forced out the only thing she could think of. "What?"

"Come by tomorrow," he repeated as patiently as a parent spoon-feeding a child, "and we'll talk."

"All right. Thank you." She hopped to her feet in excitement, though she knew perfectly well he couldn't see her.

"See you tomorrow, then," he murmured before they said their goodbyes and hung up.

Juliet slapped her phone down on the low coffee table, then headed back to her room. What did one wear to a meeting with a private investigator?

The only detectives she could picture were the television and pulp-fiction type—*Magnum, P.I.,* Sam Spade, *Columbo.* But somehow she couldn't imagine showing up in a hibiscus-covered blouse or '30s-style dress and wide-brim hat.

Thanks to her role at Zaccaro Fashions, her closet was bursting at the seams with clothes to choose from. Surely she could put something together by tomorrow morning.

As she fingered through hangers and studied her shoe choices, she found herself pushing aside Mr. McCormack's assertion that he might not be able to help her find Lily, letting herself believe that he not only could, but *would.*

Five

Lily arrived at Ashdown Abbey bright and early the next morning—but not without a struggle. She'd only gotten about four hours of sleep before her alarm had rudely awakened her and forced her back into the land of the living.

Gulping down her third cup of coffee since reaching the office, Lily sat at her desk and prayed she would be able to hold her composure when Nigel stepped off the elevator.

After saying good-night and slipping into her apartment, she'd gone to the bedroom and changed into a pair of simple cotton pajamas, then returned to the living room with all of the printouts and information she'd managed to sneak out of Ashdown Abbey earlier.

Her movements had been so calm and deliberate. Robotic. Because underneath it all, she was a beehive of confusing thoughts and conflicting emotions.

She was *not* in Los Angeles to have her hormones go haywire just because she was in close proximity to a handsome, charming Brit. He was supposed to be her *enemy,* for heaven's sake.

But her hormones *were* going wild, distracting her and throwing her off her well-planned-out path.

Not just because Nigel was an attractive man. She'd met handsome men before. Met them, worked with them, dated and even slept with a few.

Good looks were nice, but she wasn't so weak that they could push her over the edge into total stupidity. Nor could a thick British accent, no matter how toe-curling it might be.

No, there was something else about Nigel that had her pulse thrumming and her head spinning like a kaleidoscope.

She actually kind of liked him so far, despite her preconceived notions of who Nigel Statham must be—a rich, entitled CEO, not above stealing another designer's ideas to advance his own agenda.

But would a rich, entitled thief ask her opinion on something as important as hiring choices and then actually *listen* to her answer? Would he compliment her on her insight and walk her to her door at the end of the evening?

The worst part, though, was the kiss. A simple kiss on the cheek, not much different than she'd received a thousand times from older acquaintances, uncles, even her own father.

Then again, it was *so* not like a kiss from her father. Light and on the cheek, yes. To anyone who might have been watching, it would have seemed to be exactly what it was—a polite, friendly good-night kiss. A thanks-for-a-nice-evening, take-care, sleep-tight kiss from one friend to another. Or in this case, a man to a woman he'd only recently met.

But Lily knew differently. Or at least she *felt* differently. Never before had a simple kiss on the cheek caused her temperature to rise. Her heartbeat to kick into a gallop. Her stomach to launch into a series of somersaults that would put an Olympic gymnast to shame.

And that was all at only the first touch of his lips on her skin.

She'd expected him to pull away almost immediately. A quick peck, that's all. It was almost what she'd hoped for, because then her vitals would return to normal.

For some reason, though, he'd lingered. Not long enough for the moment to become awkward, but certainly long enough for everything in her to turn warm and liquid, and for her chest to tighten as she held her breath.

One-one thousand.

Two-one thousand.

Three-one thousand.

She'd begun to count silently, the way she and her sisters had when they were young, playing hide-and-seek. Until she worried that lack of oxygen might start to make her light-headed.

And then he'd pulled away. Straightening to his full height, and gazing at her with an intensity that sent a shiver down her spine.

Murmuring another quick, mumbled goodbye, he'd turned on his heel and marched away.

He'd gone, but the aftereffects of the kiss had remained. Through the rest of the night and into this morning.

She could swear she still felt the brush of his mouth against her cheek even now.

And wasn't that going to be a terrific way to go through the day? Imagining ghost lips dancing along her skin. Wondering if the look she'd seen in Nigel's eyes just before he'd walked away had been desire…or distaste.

Taking another long swig of coffee, she let the strong, hot brew slide down her throat and trickle into her system. A caffeine IV would be better. Then again, so would a nice shot of vodka. Or maybe a splash of whiskey to make the coffee both smoother and more potent.

Fingers flexing around the ceramic mug, Lily told herself to stop being so flighty. She wasn't here—in Los Angeles or at Ashdown Abbey—to daydream or wax poetic. And she certainly needed to get her act together before Nigel arrived.

Thoughts of that stupid kiss and what it might or might not mean had kept her up half the night. They didn't need to distract her all day, too. Especially since she had much more important things to focus on.

One was pretending to be the perfect personal assistant for Nigel.

The other was digging and snooping to see what else she could find concerning her stolen designs.

She'd gone through the California Collection design print-outs as much as she could last night before finally succumbing to exhaustion and crawling into bed, but she could barely remember a thing about them now. A second and possibly even third run-through was definitely called for. Of course, she couldn't do that until tonight when she was home and alone again.

A few yards down the hall, she heard the hum of the elevator and the whoosh of the doors as they opened and closed. Rushing to set aside her coffee, Lily took a deep breath, straightened in her chair, and started typing nothing in particular in an effort to look busy.

Nigel spotted Lillian the minute he stepped off the lift onto his office floor. If it was possible, she looked even more lovely today than she had last evening, and she'd looked quite stunning then.

Perhaps because he'd always had a bit of a soft spot for the "sexy librarian" type. Her hair was pulled back in a sexy bun, bookish, dark-rimmed glasses resting on the bridge of her nose. Her jewelry was understated. She wore a red blouse that opened at the throat to reveal just enough pale flesh and shadowed cleavage to make a man's libido sit up and take notice.

She was seated behind her desk, so he couldn't tell what she was wearing from the waist down. What he imagined, though, was tight and formfitting, showing off her legs and posterior to perfection. On top of that, he imagined her perching on the edge of the desk, legs crossed, shoe dangling from the toe of one foot, nibbling seductively on the end of her pen.

Oh, yes—naughty librarian, indeed. Or more to the point, naughty secretary. Which was the thought that had plagued him all through last night.

An affair with his secretary was not only bad form, but an extremely bad idea in general. As was allowing himself to be distracted by ungentlemanly and very un-bosslike thoughts about her.

He'd spent an inordinate amount of time unable to sleep, kept awake by memories of their dinner together and that kiss at her door just before saying their good-nights.

For a kiss akin to one he might give his mother or a beloved aunt, it had rocked him back on his heels and made him sorry he had to walk away.

Worse, though, was that the thought of that one simple kiss on the cheek had snowballed into a thousand other thoughts and images he had no business thinking.

Lillian perched on the edge of her desk, shoe dangling from her toes was only the first of many. The wee hours of the night had also been filled with more erotic fantasies.

Pressing Lillian up against the door to her flat and kissing her for real. On the mouth, with lips and tongue and unbridled passion.

Walking her backward into her flat and taking her on whatever surface they bumped into first. Table, counter, sofa, coffee table…even the floor itself.

Bringing her home with him and making love to her in his

own bed. On satin sheets, with moonlight streaming across their naked bodies and bringing out the highlights in her dark blond hair.

The one that was bound to cause him the most trouble, however, was of watching her saunter into his office under the pretense of work, only to have him strip her of those sexy schoolmarm eyeglasses, pull the pins from her upswept hair and shag her brains out in the middle of his desk.

It was the single, red-hot thought spiraling through his mind and making it decidedly uncomfortable to walk the remaining distance to his office. She lifted her head as he approached, and he hoped to heaven she didn't notice the state of his arousal behind the zip of his otherwise pressed and pristine trousers.

"Good morning," she greeted him.

If her smile seemed a bit stiff or falsely bright, he pretended not to notice. She wasn't the only one feeling awkward and uncomfortable over whatever had passed between them last night.

"Good morning," he returned without inflection, studiously avoiding eye contact while he reached for the morning's post on the corner of her desk and flipped through.

"Coffee?" she asked.

"No, thank you."

Her smile slipped, uncertainty skating like clouds across the sky-blue of her eyes.

Nigel blew out a breath. He was being a bleeding sod, and he knew it. It wasn't her fault that he'd gotten very little sleep and woken up about ten feet to the left of the wrong side of the bed.

"I would love a cup of tea, though," he said in a much kinder voice.

She nodded quickly and rose, going around him and her

desk to the small pantry that was tucked away at the far side of the reception area.

He watched her cross the expanse, her long legs eating up the space in record time. The slant of her three-inch, open-toed shoes made those legs look even longer, more taut. And her skirt—which turned out to be short and black—encased her buttocks like a second skin.

Not exactly conducive to quelling his arousal. The only thing that might help with that was distance. And possibly being struck blind.

Since the latter wasn't likely to occur in the next few minutes, he opted for the former. Taking the stack of envelopes with him, he moved into his office and took a seat behind his desk.

He'd just logged on to check his email when Lillian appeared carrying a full tea service—the one he'd ordered when he'd first come to work in the States, but hadn't seen hide nor hair of since. When he'd requested a cup of tea from his previous assistants, they'd all brought him a big, clunky ceramic mug with a nondescript tea bag bobbing in a pool of lukewarm water.

Nigel sat back, waiting while she set the tray on the edge of his desk and proceeded to pour already steeped tea from a china pot into a china cup. Through a stainless-steel strainer and complete with matching saucer, no less.

"This is a surprise," he said.

She raised her head, meeting his gaze. The question was there in her eyes.

"I was expecting something much simpler," he explained. "Aren't you Americans fond of tea that comes in bags?"

"We are," she answered. "Very. Probably because it's a lot easier than all of this." She waved a hand to encompass the tray and its accoutrements. "But I've heard you Brits are much more particular about your tea. And that you don't think we Americans could brew a decent cup to save our lives."

His lips quirked with the urge to grin. "We sound like a demanding lot with sticks up our bums."

Lillian chuckled, returning her attention to the tea service. "You said it, I didn't," she replied, handing him the cup and saucer.

"To be safe, I went online and researched how to make a cup of *true* English tea. I make absolutely no promises that I've done it right, but I do hope you'll at least give me points for trying."

Gesturing to the other items on the tray, she said, "Milk, sugar and lemon."

The real thing, he noticed. Milk—not cream, which so many Americans assumed should be added just because they used it in their coffee—the sugar cubed and the lemon cut into wedges.

"I wasn't sure which, if any, you preferred."

"If this tastes as good as it looks, I may even give you a bonus," he told her. "For future reference, though, I take it black, so all the rest isn't really necessary."

She blinked, looking at him as though he'd said he wasn't actually British, it was all just a cruel hoax.

"Then *why* do you have a full tea service in the kitchenette? I bought all of this specifically so you could have tea just the way you like it and wouldn't be disappointed."

He bit back a grin, but had the dignity to flush at her chastisement. "Truthfully, it came that way, as a set. My mother has used a full tea service from the time I was a lad, so I suppose it never occurred to me that I really only needed the pot, cups and saucers."

With a huff, she dropped into one of the soft leather chairs opposite his desk and crossed one leg over the other. Her skirt shifted, revealing inches more of stocking-clad skin that he shouldn't be staring at. But he couldn't seem to drag his gaze away until he'd looked his fill.

Licking suddenly dry lips, he swallowed and drew his attention—reluctantly—to her face.

"I apologize for misleading you."

"But I worked really hard on getting this right, and now I find out I could have just dropped a tea bag into a cup of hot water and been done with it," she said, still sounding put out.

He inclined his head, acknowledging her upset. "I understand. My fault entirely. Feel free to do exactly that from now on. It may not be my preference, but it's no less than I deserve."

She studied him for a moment, blue eyes locked on his. Then she leaned back, almost deflating into her chair.

"You're not what I expected, you know," she said finally, surprising him with her boldness.

He cocked a brow. "Oh? How so?"

"I thought you would be a bit more demanding. Dictatorial, even. Like that chef on the cooking show who yells all the time and calls the contestants names."

Nigel couldn't help but chuckle. He knew exactly who she was talking about. "Actually, I believe he's Scottish, not British. And I don't recall ever calling anyone a donkey, no matter how angry I might have been."

"Good thing," she replied matter-of-factly. "I don't think you'd appreciate my reaction if you used a term like that with me."

"I can imagine." He could, and it wasn't pretty. Of course, he'd never been one to get red in the face and start slinging invectives when he lost his temper, so she had nothing to worry about on that score.

"You're not at all what I expected, either," he confessed.

He regretted the words as soon as they passed his lips. It

was a bit too much sharing for their short acquaintance, not to mention entirely out of character for him.

Of course, she'd heard him, so it wasn't as though he could pretend he hadn't said it.

She tipped her head to one side, glancing at him curiously. "You mean you thought I'd be quieter, more tractable, eager to please."

Nigel chuckled aloud at that description. Despite the fact that she had, indeed, seemed eager to please her new boss in the two days she'd been in his employ, something told him that wasn't entirely usual for her, and that the rest didn't suit her by half.

Quiet? Not if by that she meant meek.

Tractable? He couldn't imagine any such thing.

"No," he answered, giving his head a rather decisive shake. "Not at all. Given the past assistants I've had here in the U.S., I was expecting you to be…a few biscuits short of a tin, if you understand my meaning."

"You're in the habit of hiring mentally unstable personal assistants?" she teased, brow raised.

"Not unstable, thank goodness," he responded, "but young, and not a lot going on above the neck, other than good grooming and dreams of becoming either a supermodel or the next fashion designer to become an overnight success. Not only could they not make a decent cup of tea, but they couldn't keep their minds on their responsibilities long enough to accomplish what they'd actually been hired to do."

She thought about that for a moment, then inclined her head and her gaze toward the cup still resting on the desk in front of him.

"You haven't even tasted the tea yet. How do you know *I* can make a decent cup?"

He didn't bother to answer, simply lifted the cup to his mouth and took a long, hearty swallow. Setting the cup back down, he said, "Excellent. It would have been better if I'd started drinking it while it was still piping hot, but really—quite excellent."

"Well, you have only yourself to blame for that, don't you?" she quipped.

Without a hint of remorse or fear of speaking in such a manner to her employer. And not just any employer, but the CEO of the whole bloody company.

Why did that amuse him so damn much? Amuse, as well as arouse.

The sight of her, the thought of her, the knowledge that she would be seated just outside his office door for eight hours each day, was enough to send his blood to the boiling point.

Even now, he wanted to stand up, round his desk, lean down and kiss her just for the hell of it.

Well, for the hell of it, and also to discover if she tasted as good as he thought she would. That was something he suddenly wanted to know. Very, very badly.

In an attempt to cool the heat rising in his body and bringing small beads of perspiration to dot his brow, he raised the tea back to his lips and drained the cup dry. It didn't cool him off as much as he'd hoped.

"So," he commented to fill the increasingly awkward silence. "You can make a fine cup of tea, and you know your way about the design business—at least judging by last night's conversation. I think it's safe to say you've already surpassed the skills of all of my other assistants here in the States put together."

"I'll take that as a compliment," she replied, giving him a bright smile that Nigel believed could only be genuine.

So he responded with one of his own. "As you should. It was intended as one."

"I can expect that bonus to be reflected in my first paycheck, then?"

She made it a question. Loaded and dangerous.

Narrowing his eyes, he answered carefully. "We'll see. Keep up the good work, and I'll have no problem rewarding your efforts monetarily. But you've only been here two days. I need to see you in action awhile longer than that before I make any promises."

She shrugged one slim shoulder. "Can't blame a girl for trying."

With a laugh, Nigel emptied the rest of the tea into his cup, then sat back, linking his hands in front of him. "Certainly not. And you may just earn yourself some extra perks yet. Especially if you bring me another pot of tea before running down to the fourth floor to see how things are going. We've got a special runway show coming up in two weeks, and I want to be sure we're on track."

Lillian sat up in a suddenly more serious, alert manner. "I'll be happy to, but isn't that something you should do yourself? I'm not sure I'll know enough to judge how well things are going."

"You'll do fine," Nigel assured her. "The head of the design team should be able to tell you what's been done so far and what still needs to be taken care of. Then you can report to me, and if I think anything is out of sorts, I'll go down and put the fear of unemployment into them."

"Very stealthy of you," she said. Then, taking a deep breath, she pushed to her feet. "I'll do my best. It will be fun to visit the design-room floor. I've never been on one before."

Her gaze darted away and she shifted from one leg to the other. Peculiar, to say the least.

Ignoring the odd behavior, Nigel said, "Take your time down there. It really is quite fascinating to watch the designers work."

She nodded, collecting the china cup from the center of

the desk and adding it to the other items on the tea-service tray. Gathering it all, she headed for the door.

"Tea first," she said over her shoulder, "then I'll go down and spy on your happy little elves."

He watched her disappear out into the reception area, enjoying the sway of her hips and straight line of her back. It wasn't until he heard her returning with a second cup of tea several minutes later that he realized he hadn't moved a muscle since she'd walked away.

Which was not a good sign. Not good at all.

Six

Lily knew better than to make rash judgments about people. First impressions often made you think somebody was wonderful, friendly, trustworthy…and then later you discovered they were none of those things. Other times, the opposite was true. You met someone and didn't care for them at all, only to discover hidden aspects of their personality later that caused you to end up becoming close friends.

So the fact that she was finding Nigel Statham more handsome, more charming and more enticing the longer she knew him—even after only two short days—could go either way. She'd started out certain he was a thief with questionable business ethics. Could she have been completely and totally wrong about that? Or was she letting his intense good looks and honeyed accent blind her to the truth?

She'd expected to come to Los Angeles, go to work for the big, bad CEO of the U.S. branch of his family's company and immediately begin finding evidence to shore up her arguments about his involvement in the theft of her designs.

Instead, she'd found nothing. None of her poking around in his files—or his former personal assistants' files, at any rate—had turned up a single thing or question mark. If anything, she was less convinced of his involvement.

But the theft *had* occurred, so there had to be evidence somewhere. A thread she could find, pick at and follow back to its source.

The elevator she was riding down to the fourth floor stopped with a small jolt and she straightened, pushing away from the rear wall where she'd been leaning to wait for the doors to open.

She'd lied to Nigel when she'd told him she'd never visited a design-room floor before. Sometimes she felt as though she lived on one, especially when she and both of her sisters were in their home studio together, all working in tandem.

Which was probably why she was so looking forward to visiting the one here. Not only was she curious to see how things worked at a company of this size, but it would be comforting to be back in the thick of the creative side of the fashion business again. Even temporarily.

As she stepped off the elevator, the click of her heels on the slick polished floor mixed with the sound of voices and the hum of sewing machines. Not a dozen running all at once, but one here, one there, being used as needed, much the way they were in her shop.

She loved it. A noise that would probably grate on anyone else's nerves after a while soothed hers and helped her to take her first deep, comfortable breath since leaving New York.

She was smiling as she made her way down the main hall. This floor was made up of large, open-area rooms filled with long tables, dress forms, sewing equipment and plenty of fabrics and supplies. And most of the rooms she passed had their doors open so she could see the people working inside. Design teams, most likely, each assigned a different look or aspect of whatever collection they were currently putting together.

What Lily wouldn't give for this kind of setup. Not only the work space—which was like comparing a football field to a foosball table—but the employees. Extra creative minds, extra hands, twice or probably even quadruple the work accomplished in half the time.

Of course, in order to put something like this into effect, she would also need a lot more money. And that would mean either asking her parents for another, more substantial loan, or winning the lottery.

But a girl could dream, couldn't she? And one day, Zaccaro Fashions *would* be this big, this efficient. They would be a huge, world-renowned brand name in their own right, and she wouldn't need her future inheritance to make it happen.

She wanted to stop at each doorway and take a good, long peek inside. She wanted to know what everyone was making, see their work, listen in on their conversations. Especially since it was possible they were once again ripping off her designs.

There wasn't a lot of time for poking around, though. She was supposed to find a man named Michael Franklin, the head designer for this particular collection, and get a progress report for Nigel.

Despite his comment that she should take her time, she didn't trust him not to come looking for her. He was a big, corporate bigwig who didn't even make his own coffee or tea. What were the chances he could get through an hour or two without needing her for something?

And he was quite obviously a man who expected his assistant to come running the minute he called…even if she was three floors away. So the less time she spent away from

...er desk the better, at least until she'd been at the company a little longer and had a better handle on his routine.

Strolling down the hall, she took in the activities of each ...oom peripherally as she passed, heading straight for the of...ice at the end, where Nigel had told her she would most likely ...ind Mr. Franklin. Or at least it was a place to start.

"Office" was a bit of a misnomer. It was actually a glass-fronted version of the other design areas, but in addition to ...quipment and a cutting table that doubled as a sketching and ...esign surface, there was a cluttered desk and file cabinets.

Mr. Franklin's name was etched on the closed door, but no ...ne was inside. Chewing the inside of her lip for a second, she ...apped her foot and tried to decide what to do next. Her only ...ption, she supposed, was to go back the way she'd come and ...op her head into each room after all. Surely someone would ...ave an idea of where she could find Mr. Franklin.

She was spinning on her heel to do just that when she ...early ran into another woman coming toward her.

"Oh, I'm so sorry."

Their simultaneous apologies were followed by amused ...huckles.

"Sorry about that," the woman said again. "I saw you ...tanding outside Mr. Franklin's office and was just coming ...o ask if I could help you with anything."

"I'm looking for Mr. Franklin, actually," Lily said. And ...hen she stopped, tipping her head and narrowing her eyes as ...he concentrated more intently on the other woman.

"Wait a minute. Don't I know you?" She wracked her brain, ...ositive the young woman looked familiar.

"Oh, my gosh," she exclaimed as it finally came to her. "You're Bella, aren't you? I'm sorry, I can't think of your last ...ame off the top of my head, but you're Zoe's friend, aren't ...you? Her roommate from college."

"It's Landry," the other woman, who was a petite brunette,

supplied. And then she widened her cornflower-blue eyes. "Do you mean Zoe Zaccaro?"

Lily nodded.

"I haven't seen Zoe in ages, but we definitely spent our college years together. How do you know her?"

"I'm Lily, Zoe's sister. We met briefly the last time you visited Zoe in New York."

She wasn't surprised at Bella's lack of recognition. Normally, she and her sisters looked enough alike—with their long, blond hair and similar facial features—that they were often mistaken for one another. But with her hair both darkened and pulled up in an out-of-character twist, and unfamiliar glasses perched on the bridge of her nose, she'd done a pretty good job of muting all of the things that made her stand out as a Zaccaro by looks alone.

Not to mention that she hadn't seen Bella in years—and had only met her a couple of times before that, when they had visited Zoe on campus or Zoe had brought Bella home with her for the odd holiday break.

"Oh, yes. Wow, small world. It's great to see you again. And how is Zoe?" Bella asked.

"Great," Lily told her. "Same as usual."

They both laughed at that, aware of exactly what Zoe's "usual" was.

"So what are you doing here?" Bella wanted to know.

The question stopped Lily cold, slapping the smile right off her face. Uh-oh. Until then, she'd forgotten she was supposed to be keeping a low profile and *definitely* remaining anonymous to everyone who worked at Ashdown Abbey. She had forgotten while exchanging pleasantries with a friend of her sister's whom she'd run into out of the blue.

Mind racing, she tried to figure out how to cover her mistake and come up with a plausible reason for her presence here in Los Angeles.

"The three of us are, um…taking a little time off from de-
signing, working to establish the store and brand as they are
now. So while Zoe and Juliet are running things back home,
I decided to come out here and intern with Ashdown Abbey
for a while."

That sounded okay, didn't it? She very pointedly didn't
mention that she was working as the big kahuna's assistant.
And she hoped Bella didn't find out, because then she would
have to explain why she was going by a different name and
pray they never ran into one another while Nigel was around.

"Cool," Bella replied, apparently accepting Lily's explanation at face value.

"How about you?" Lily asked, eager to turn the younger
woman's attention away from her and on to something, anything else.

"Oh, I'm, um…" Bella stammered, glancing down at the
toes of her pointy, leopard-print shoes before returning her
gaze to Lily, but not quite meeting her eyes. "I'm an associate
designer for the company," she said finally. "I've been here
for almost three years now."

"That's wonderful," Lily told her, meaning it. She didn't
know Bella well, wasn't even sure how long she and Zoe had
been friends, but she'd never heard her sister speak a bad word
about her, and she seemed perfectly nice.

"You're working on the latest collection, then?" she asked,
nodding her head to indicate all of the fourth-floor workrooms.

Bella gave a jerky nod, her gaze skating away again for
the briefest of moments. "I don't really have much to do with
it. I'm just sort of a cog in the wheel, doing a little here and
a little there. Whatever needs to be done."

"Hey, you have to start somewhere," Lily said with a pleas-
ant smile, knowing the truth of that better than anyone. "I'm

sure it will be great. All of Ashdown Abbey's designs are ex
ceptional. You should be proud to be a part of it."

That was true, too, even if it pained her to say so. Espe
cially since she was still smarting from their use of *her* grea
designs for their California Collection.

She thought about trying to wheedle information from
Bella—about the California Collection, or Nigel, or maybe
just Ashdown Abbey itself. It was possible she knew some
thing important without even being aware of it. But after
blurting out her real identity when she was supposed to be
undercover, she was afraid of coming across as too curious
and giving herself away even further, so she kept her mouth
shut. She could always come back later to pick Bella's brain
if she needed to.

It also crossed her mind that—being a friend of Zoe's and
having been in their studio in the past—Bella might have had
something to do with the theft of her designs. She didn't want
to believe that a friend of her sister's—especially one who'd
roomed with Zoe for four years straight—would do such a
thing, but made a mental note to look into it anyway. At least
cursorily, just in case.

"Do you know where Mr. Franklin is?" she asked instead
of beginning an impromptu interrogation right there in the
hallway.

Bella glanced back over her shoulder. "Um…he should be
here somewhere. Try workroom B. He's been working pretty
closely with that team this week."

"Great, thank you."

"Do you want me to take you?" Bella offered, finally mak
ing eye contact.

"No, thanks. I can find it, and I'm sure you have work to
do," Lily said. "It was nice to see you, though. I'll tell Zoe
you said hi."

After saying their goodbyes, Bella headed in one direction

while Lily retraced her path toward the elevator. She went more slowly this time, figuring she had a valid excuse for poking her head into each room to see who was there and what was going on. So what if workroom B was one of the last rooms she'd pass?

She caught glimpses of the color palette and fabrics that were being used for this particular collection, as well as a few of the designs themselves being pieced together on dress forms. Lily liked what she saw, and so far, at least, she hadn't spotted anything that set off alarm bells in her head. Nothing that looked eerily similar to her own design aesthetic.

It was a relief, but also a touch disappointing, since it got her no closer to finding out how her designs had been stolen in the first place.

Since she didn't see anyone in the other workrooms who seemed to be in charge, she decided to wait until she reached workroom B to ask after Mr. Franklin. She could always backtrack later if she needed to.

Reaching workroom B, she stepped inside, taking in the two women bent over a cutting table, heads together in discussion, and another woman over by a dress form, talking with a short, squat man while they fingered pieces of a pattern already attached to the form, moving them around and trying to decide on the best placement.

She might have been jumping to conclusions, but Lily assumed the man was Mr. Franklin. Sidling just a few feet more into the room, she leaned against one of the cutting tables and studied some of the patterns and sketches laid out there while she waited for them to conclude their business so she could get Nigel's update and report back to him before he sent out a search party.

The next week went by in such a blur, Lily could barely keep up. Nigel kept her running, skipping and hopping nearly twenty-four/seven.

Even once she clocked out and dragged herself to her home away from home, she had enough energy only to wash her face, change into pajamas and fall into bed for as much sleep as she could manage before the alarm went off and demanded she start all over again. Which left very little time for snooping and research.

She was gaining a whole new respect for secretaries, receptionists and personal assistants, to be sure.

And even though she was often left scrambling or faking her way through certain tasks, Nigel seemed pleased with her performance. So she supposed if the "design thing"—as her father sometimes called it—didn't work out, she could always fall back on this.

But she wasn't here to work hard and see that Ashdown Abbey's CEO looked good so the company could advance. She was here to save and avenge *her* company, and she was becoming increasingly frustrated with her inability to do that.

More determined than ever to find a moment or two to poke around for her own benefit, Lily stalked out of the elevator first thing that Monday morning and went straight to her desk. She'd arrived a tad early, and with luck, Nigel would run late this morning so she could dig into the California Collection files without fear of getting caught.

There had to be something somewhere that would lead her to the culprit she sought. She was especially interested in finding the original sketches that the California Collection was based off of. They should give her more of an indication of what inspired the collection than the later, more cleaned-up versions she'd already printed. They might even give her some hint of how someone got ahold of her designs in the first place to mimic them.

Of course, her lack of progress with her private little investigation wasn't the only dilemma she was facing. She also had a real private investigator breathing down her neck.

Reid McCormack had called to ask where she was and what she was up to. She'd found the question and his tone of voice peculiar, since he was the one who was supposed to be working for her.

But while she'd hired him to see what he could find out about Ashdown Abbey's theft of Zaccaro Fashions' designs from his vantage point in New York, she hadn't told him that she was planning to head for Los Angeles to do a bit of investigating on her own. She doubted he would approve, and suspected he would only try to talk her out of it.

She was right about the disapproval part. He'd been as livid as a person could be over the phone when it wasn't his place to tell her what to do—or what not to do—and he knew it.

He'd wanted to know *exactly* where she was and *exactly* what she was doing. Then when she'd refused to tell him, he'd informed her that "whatever she was up to," she obviously wasn't doing a very good job of it because her sister—Juliet— had just come to his office asking him to track her down.

Lily had gotten the feeling he was more put out at having to lie to one sister because the other was already a client than anything else. And maybe that he'd been blindsided, not even knowing client number one had hied off on her own until potential client number two came along wanting her sister treated like a missing person.

Though she'd hoped Juliet and Zoe would trust her to go off on her own for a while without needing specifics, she apparently hadn't done as efficient a job as she'd thought of making excuses, assuring her sisters she was fine and would return home soon.

It had taken a long time and quite a bit of verbal tap dancing to finally convince Mr. McCormack to pretend to take Juliet's case. Lily offered to compensate him for his time on both issues, if he didn't feel comfortable taking money from Juliet for doing nothing and lying to her to boot. And it was only until she could figure out what to say to her sisters that wouldn't send them into a tailspin. She promised to call Juliet herself as soon as she could so her family wouldn't continue to think she was missing or in trouble.

It went against McCormack's personal code of ethics, she could tell. She could almost imagine him grinding his teeth, flexing his fingers over and over again, and generally fighting the urge to reach through the phone line to strangle her.

Eventually, though...*eventually*, he agreed. About as enthusiastically as one might say, "Oh, yes—please give me a root canal without anesthetic!"

So now that was hanging over her head, as well. She hated thinking that her sisters were worried about her, especially when she'd left a note with the sole purpose of making sure they didn't.

But if she called to reassure them again and let them know everything was okay, they—namely Juliet—would want to know where she was and what was going on. They would be more curious and demanding than ever. And she had no idea what to tell them.

With a sigh, she dropped down into the chair at her desk and punched the power button on the computer. While it was booting up, she stowed her purse and tried to figure out where to begin. The sooner she could get this mess cleaned up and the mystery solved, the sooner she could go home and tell her sisters everything.

She tapped at the keyboard, searching folder and file names, looking specifically for anything related to the California Collection while keeping one eye on the elevator down the hall.

Though she wasn't sure it would lead anywhere, she discovered a folder that seemed to have all kinds of documents in it related to the California Collection. As quickly as she could, she slipped a blank flash drive into the USB port and hit Copy.

The file had just finished loading, and she was dropping the flash drive into her purse, when the door to Nigel's office opened directly behind her.

Her heart stopped. Literally screeched to a halt inside her chest as a lump of pure panic formed in her throat.

"Good. You're here," Nigel murmured at her back.

She knew she should respond, at least turn around and face him, but she felt glued in place, as frozen as an ice cube.

Thankfully, rather than getting upset or reprimanding her for her seeming lack of respect, he came to the edge of her desk. When the dark blue pinstripe of his dress slacks came into her peripheral vision, she finally managed to swallow, turn her head and lift her gaze to that of her boss.

As always, the sight of him made her mouth go dry. She'd thought that after working with him for a while, getting used to his quiet confidence and startling good looks, it would get easier to be around him. That she would suffer less and less of a lurch to her solar plexus each time they came in contact—which was more often, even, than she caught her own reflection in the restroom mirror.

Heart beating again—though not in any pattern a cardiologist would approve of—she licked her lips and made herself meet his eyes.

"Good morning," she said, glad her voice sounded almost human. "I didn't think you were in yet."

Understatement. She'd been watching the elevator like a mouse on the lookout for the cat of the house. Meanwhile, he'd been in his office the entire time. If he'd been a cat and she a mouse, she was pretty sure she'd be lunch by now.

"I was waiting for you to arrive," he said by way of answer. Pushing aside a few items on the corner of her desk, he sat down, letting one leg dangle. A nicely muscled leg, encased in fabric that tightened across his upper thigh.

Once again dragging her gaze to his face, she tried to take slow, shallow breaths until her internal temperature stopped climbing toward heatstroke levels.

"We need to talk about next week's show," he continued.

"All right." He'd sent her down to speak with Michael Franklin several more times, but to the best of her knowledge, everything was still running smoothly and on schedule.

"As you know, the show is in Miami."

She had known that, though she hadn't paid much attention one way or the other to the show's location.

"I have to be there, of course," he said in that slow, calm British way of his. Whatever point he was trying to make, he was taking his time getting there.

"The runway show itself is for charity, but buyers for many of our biggest accounts will be there, and we'll be taking orders for the designs throughout the event."

She nodded in understanding.

"I was hoping you might be willing to go along, as well."

Lily's eyes widened and she sat back in her seat, more than a little surprised by the request. They'd been discussing the show on and off since her arrival, but he'd never once hinted that he might want her to travel across the country with him.

"Do your personal assistants normally travel with you for this sort of thing?" she wanted to know.

He inclined his head. "Quite often."

"Then you're *telling* me I'll be going along, not asking if I'd like to," she said, making it more of a statement than a question.

"Not at all," he replied quickly, shifting on the corner of her desk. "I'd very much like you to accompany me, and it will be work-related, but I'll certainly understand if you have other plans."

She thought about it, trying to weigh the pros and cons and mentally map out the best plan of action where her true purpose for working at Ashdown Abbey was concerned.

On the one hand, she would probably make more progress and have more privacy to really dig around if she stayed behind while Nigel flew to Miami.

On the other, she *really* wanted to go. The idea of traveling with Nigel—no doubt first-class all the way—was intriguing enough. But the true thrill would be the up-close-and-personal experience of a live show with numerous famous designers sending their latest creations down the runway.

She could really benefit from watching how the organizers pulled it together and getting to see how such a large-scale event worked behind the scenes. Watching the clothes walk down the runway on professional and likely very sought-after supermodels. Rubbing elbows with some of the biggest names in the business—designers, buyers and the media alike. People who might one day take an interest in her own designs and help Zaccaro Fashions go national and then international.

Granted, she wouldn't be able to let any of them know who she really was or talk up her own work, but still… The contacts she might make, even under the guise of acting as Nigel's personal assistant, could serve her well down the road.

"It will be an overnight stay," Nigel added, breaking into her thoughts to give her even more to consider. "Through the weekend, actually. We'd fly out Thursday and return late Sunday night."

It was a substantial amount of time to be away from the Ashdown Abbey offices and attempt to carry out her pretense in public, but was she really going to say no? Pass up such an amazing opportunity? She would never be able to live with herself if she did, despite the fact that it would set back her "investigation" by that much longer.

"I'd love to go," she said after a minute of deep thought,

relieved when the words came out normally instead of sounding like those of a kid standing outside a bouncy castle.

"Brilliant," he exclaimed, slapping the palms of his hands against the tops of both thighs.

Then he rose and headed back toward his office. "You can check my schedule for the specific itinerary and the promotional materials for the show to get an idea of what you might like to pack. We'll work out the rest of the details later."

With that, he disappeared behind the solid wooden door separating their two work areas, leaving her alone once again.

Knowing he was there meant she couldn't risk doing any more snooping. Especially since she'd learned the scary way that he could pop out at any moment rather than relying on the phone or intercom to address her.

She should have been annoyed, but was suddenly too excited. Now she had Miami to look forward to.

It was a detour, and would definitely put her behind on the whole find-the-thief-and-get-the-heck-back-to-New York thing. But it was *Miami,* for heaven's sake.

Not just Miami the city. She'd been there several times before, as well as Key West and one ill-fated trip to Daytona Beach that her parents still didn't know about. And with luck, they never, ever would.

No, it was Miami during the event of the season—at least one of them, as far as the fashion world was concerned. A number of labels, not just Ashdown Abbey, would be flaunting their latest designs during what had become a very high-profile annual show.

The show itself—Fashion for a Cause—raised money for a different charity each year. This time, it was for a children's hospital. But the one-of-a-kind fashions that were shown at the event were then mass-produced and began to show up in retail outlets across the country and even around the world, depending on orders received during and soon after their debuts at the show.

Lily and her sisters were nowhere near the level one needed to achieve to participate in this type of event. She'd never even attended, though it had always been a distant, hopeful dream.

Now she had the chance to go. Not just as a member of the audience twelve rows back, but as Nigel Statham's girl Friday.

It was kind of a thrill. One that could quickly turn into a nightmare, if her true identity was discovered, but she was pretty sure it was worth the risk. Even after bumping into Bella Landry, no one had looked at her differently or started asking pointed questions about her presence, so she still seemed to be safe.

In fact, during a bit of digging into Bella's association with Ashdown Abbey, she'd actually learned that the young woman had just requested a bit of personal time from work. Lily intended to look into that, see if there was any more to it than sick days or a short vacation, but hadn't yet had the chance.

But with luck, her obscurity at the company would continue.

And she was almost giddy with anticipation about the charity show, so…yeah, she was going to take the chance. Wear giant sunglasses, introduce herself under her assumed name and hope for the best.

Too excited to simply sit there, she accessed Nigel's daily schedule and zipped ahead to the dates of the Miami trip. It looked as though they would be gone four days and three nights. Flying on the corporate jet. Staying in the luxury suites of the Royal Crown Hotel, one of the most expensive hotel chains on the East Coast.

As excited as she was about the runway show itself, she wondered if there would be time to slip away for a massage and spa treatment. Lord knew the amenities at the Royal Crown had to be amazing.

Like any good PA, she needed to start making a list. Of everything she would need to pack for herself, but also whatever business-related items she—or more specifically, Nigel—might need.

Clothing-wise, she knew she should continue wearing garments exclusively from the Ashdown Abbey lines. But even though they did some very nice summer and activewear pieces, nothing that she'd seen so far was as ideal for the sun and surf atmosphere of Miami as her own designs.

Her lightweight fabrics, bright colors and floral prints would be perfect, absolutely perfect for such a trip. And she had several just-perfect pieces with her in California.

The question was: Did she have the courage to take them along and wear them in front of Nigel? Would he notice they weren't from the Ashdown Abbey collections and wonder about her sudden switch? Or would he write it off as simply a female thing, knowing that women tended to have overstuffed closets filled with every type of clothing for every type of occasion and very few were loyal to only one designer or label? If it looked good, fit well and—with luck—was on sale, a woman would buy it.

She sighed. It wasn't easy pretending to be a serious, buttoned-down executive secretary when all she wanted to do was rush home, kick off her shoes and blazer, let down her hair and run around packing sundresses and sandals for Miami as though it was a beach vacation rather than a short but significant business excursion.

Seven

The flight from Los Angeles to Miami was as long as it had ever been, but it passed by so smoothly, Lily couldn't have said whether it took three hours or thirty.

Nigel's—or rather, Ashdown Abbey's—corporate jet was incredible. She'd been on a Jet Stream before, but traveling with Nigel as his personal assistant was quite different from traveling with her parents and sisters for a business-slash-pleasure trip. Especially since that had been years ago, when she was much younger and harder to keep in her seat.

This time around, she was mature enough to appreciate the soft-as-butter leather seats, the interior that looked more like a *House Beautiful* living room than the inside of an airplane and the single flight attendant who appeared when she was needed, but was otherwise neither seen nor heard.

A car was waiting for them when they landed. The driver stood outside, ready to collect their bags and load them into the trunk after holding the rear door while they climbed inside the perfectly air-conditioned vehicle. Given Miami's balmy heat, Lily was grateful for the convenience.

Despite her continued misgivings, she'd opted for many of her own clothes for this particular excursion. She'd packed a couple of dark, formfitting suits, just in case, but had filled her luggage mostly with her own summer-inspired creations. Sleeveless maxi dresses that were feminine but elegant enough for the occasion, and a couple of linen skirts with light, flowy tops.

So far, Nigel didn't seem to mind her change of wardrobe, even though she'd been wearing a much darker, more subdued outfit the last time he'd seen her, and now she was sunflower bright in a short yellow dress and strappy cloth espadrilles.

The truth was, she felt much more like herself dressed this way. But since she needed to remember she wasn't *supposed* to be herself around Nigel Statham, that doing so could very well pose a problem.

She would have to be careful of what she said and how she acted—around everyone, not just Nigel—no matter what she was wearing.

When they arrived at the hotel, the driver pulled to a stop beneath the portico, then hurried around to open Nigel's door. Nigel stepped out and turned back to reach a hand in toward her.

Lily slid across the seat, putting her fingers in his as she climbed out, careful not to flash too much thigh as her dress rode up a few perilous inches.

The second they touched, a wave of heat washed over her, making the breath stutter in her chest just a bit. She tried to tell herself it was the heavy humidity hitting her as she stepped out of the air-conditioned interior of the car, but she didn't think that was true.

She'd been struck by too many unexpected hot flashes or zaps of electricity in his presence to believe they were geographical or weather-related. After all, she'd first noticed her reactions to his proximity in his office, and there had certainly been no natural humidity or direct sunlight beaming down on her there.

Avoiding Nigel's gaze in case he'd noticed the hitch in her breath, she moved away from the car while the driver and a bellman unloaded their luggage and stacked it on a waiting cart. When they finished, Nigel tipped the driver, then placed a hand at the small of her back as they followed the hotel employee inside.

Nigel had already given the bellman his name so that as they passed the registration desk, key cards were ready. All the bellman had to do was collect them, then lead the way directly to the bank of elevators that would take them to the presidential suites.

Before they'd left Los Angeles, Lily had told Nigel that just because he was staying in a luxury suite didn't mean she needed to. She could just as easily stay in a regular room, or perhaps a lower-level suite, then meet up with him whenever necessary.

Nigel wouldn't hear of it, however. He insisted that it would be more convenient to have her right next door. And besides, the reservations had already been made; no sense bothering with them now.

So even though she still thought it was an unnecessary expense, she was kind of looking forward to having an entire presidential suite to herself. It would be almost like having the entire loft back in New York to herself, which almost never happened.

The elevator carried them slowly upward, the doors opening with a quiet whoosh. The bellman stepped out with the rolling luggage cart and led them down the carpeted hallway.

At the end of it, he paused, slipped a key card into the coded lock, and let them into what was, indeed, a luxury suite.

The carpeting beneath their feet was thick and off-white, the furniture plush and chosen to match. French doors lined one entire length of the main room—facing the ocean, of course.

The view, even from across the room, was magnificent. Lily couldn't wait to get to her own suite so she could walk out onto the balcony and enjoy the soft breeze and salty sea air.

Remaining near the open door, Lily watched the bellman pull bags from the cart. When he reached for hers, though, she stepped forward and stopped him.

"Oh, no," she told him. "Those are mine. They go in my room."

The young man paused, hand still on the handle of her overnight bag. "Would you like me to carry them into the bedroom for you?" he asked, sounding slightly confused.

"No," she tried to clarify. "I'm staying in another suite. Next door, I believe."

Letting go of the bag, he checked the small paper envelope in his hand that had held the key card. "I'm sorry, ma'am, but I was only given the key to one room. Could your room be under another name?"

That drew her up short. Turning to Nigel, she cast him a questioning glance. His face was as blank as a sheet of paper.

Sensing the confusion in the room, the young man cleared his throat. "Let me call down to the front desk. I'm sure there was simply an oversight. We'll get it straightened out right away."

Crossing the room, he picked up the phone resting on the credenza beside a huge vase of freshly cut flowers. He spoke in low tones to whoever picked up on the other end.

A moment later, he hung up and turned back to them, his expression saying clearly that they weren't going to like whatever it was he had to say.

Lily's stomach tightened as she waited.

"I'm sorry, but the front desk only has one reservation under Mr. Statham's name, and none for you."

Lily exchanged another confused glance with Nigel. He shrugged a shoulder beneath the tailored lines of his charcoal suit coat.

"So we'll get a second room now. It's not a problem."

The bellman winced, and Lily knew what was coming even before he took a fortifying breath to speak. The fact that he refused to look either of them in the eye was another clear sign of impending doom.

"Unfortunately, we're fully booked. With the Fashion for a Cause event in town, just about all of the higher-end hotels are. I'm very sorry."

For several beats, no one in the room said a word, or moved a muscle for that matter. The bellman looked nervous. Nigel looked undecided. And Lily was pretty sure she looked plain old put-out.

But whatever mistake or misunderstanding had taken place, it certainly wasn't the poor hotel employee's fault.

With a sigh, Lily said, "It's all right. This suite is big enough for a family of twelve. I'm sure the two of us will be able to make do." She ended with what she hoped was a reassuring smile.

The bellman's chest dropped as he blew out a breath of relief. He thanked her profusely and finished taking their luggage off the cart, which he then rolled to the door.

Nigel followed behind, handing him what she hoped was a generous tip—hazard pay, and for nearly being sent into a panic attack—before he disappeared into the hallway.

"I'm sorry," Nigel said, strolling back to the center of the sitting area and stopping just a yard or so in front of her. "There must have been some sort of mix-up."

"I'd say so."

"My assistant normally makes these reservations for me."

She lifted a brow, silently asking if he seriously intended to blame this situation on her.

He almost—almost—cracked a smile.

"I don't usually invite my assistants to join me for these things, however, so when I asked you along, I apparently forgot to tell you we'd need to book a second room."

"Apparently," she replied drily.

Then, without another word, she turned and crossed to the large mahogany desk set against the far wall. Pulling open drawers, she found the phone book and started flipping through.

"What are you doing?" Nigel asked, moving a few feet closer.

"Looking for another hotel. A less ritzy one that might have a room available."

Reaching the desk, he leaned back against the corner nearest where she was standing, crossing his arms over his chest. "Why?"

She shot him a castigating glance. "I'm going to need somewhere to sleep. And as we've established, you only reserved one room, and this hotel is full up."

"I thought you said the suite was large enough for the both of us."

Lily kept her attention glued to the phone book, pretending her stomach hadn't just done a peculiar little somersault. In a low tone, she murmured, "I lied."

"Don't be silly," he said after a moment of tense silence.

Though she kept her gaze strictly on the yellow pages of the directory, his long, masculine fingers suddenly came into view, grasping the book at its center and plucking it from her hold.

Setting it flat on the desk behind him, he remained where he was, one palm flat on the phone book to hold it in place and stop her from snatching it back.

"There's no need for you to stay elsewhere when there's plenty of room here. Besides, as I told you before, having you at another hotel, possibly all the way across town, won't exactly be conducive to business. What if I need you for something?"

She narrowed her gaze, mimicking his earlier posture by folding her arms beneath her breasts and hitching back on one hip.

"You can call and I'll come over. I'm sure that all of the hotels in this area have working phone lines and taxis that travel in between," she told him flatly.

The specks of green in his hazel eyes flashed briefly, and Lily thought perhaps she'd gone too far. She was supposed to be his beck-and-call girl, after all, and should probably keep her sarcasm to a minimum.

"I'm afraid that's simply unacceptable," he told her, his already noticeable accent growing even thicker and more pronounced. "I don't pay you to show up when you can, I pay you to be there when I need you."

Score one for the prim-and-proper Brit, she thought.

Licking her lips, she said, "How much do you think you'll need me?" No sarcasm this time, just a straight-out question. "I was under the impression this trip would be on the light side, as far as work was concerned."

"Still," he responded without really addressing her question, "it would be better for us to stay in close proximity, just in case. Having you one door over would have been fine, but no farther than that."

Pushing away from the desk, he offered her an encouraging smile. "Don't worry, we'll make it work."

He returned to the pile of their combined luggage in the center of the room. Picking up his briefcase in one hand, laptop case in the other, he moved them to the coffee table in front of the sofa. It matched the eggshell hue of the carpet almost perfectly.

"I don't suppose this presidential suite has two bedrooms," she remarked, relaxing enough to take a few steps in his direction.

She kept her arms across her chest, though. Not tightly, but because she knew if she let her arms fall to her sides, she would only end up fidgeting.

Resigning herself to staying in the same suite as her boss was one thing. Staying in the same suite with this man, who just happened to be her temporary boss, but who also caused her mouth to go dry and other places to grow damp, was something else entirely. It made her nerves jump and dance beneath her skin.

"I don't believe so, though you're welcome to check."

More because it gave her a chance to put a little space between Nigel and herself than because she thought there was an actual chance at success, she strolled away to explore the rest of the suite.

For the most part, it had everything: a rather large kitchenette; dining and sitting areas; an entertainment area complete with television, DVD player, stereo and even a Wii; an officelike work area; and a balcony. There was a small bathroom in the main portion of the suite, but she assumed the bedroom had one of its own, as well.

And then there was the bedroom itself. Unless it somehow broke off into two separate sleeping quarters past the single doorway, there was only one. One spacious, beautiful, far-too-intimate bedroom.

Stepping over the threshold, she took in the totality of the room in a single glance. The enormous bed—a queen size, at least, but she suspected king—with the woven bamboo headboard. A low, matching bureau with an oval, almost seashell-shaped mirror attached. The small table and chair over by the sliding glass door leading to the balcony. And the open doorway that led to the master bath.

She'd been right about that, too. Apparently sparing no expense, the hotel had put in marble flooring, marble vanity, marble shower enclosure and marble tub surround. The bathtub and shower were also separate—one sunken, with jets that made her want to strip and climb in for a long, hot soak that very minute; the other the size of a compact car with an etched-glass enclosure and half a dozen nozzles arranged on the other three sides to send water spraying in all the right places.

Without a doubt, Nigel would be paying thousands of dollars a night for so many of these amazing amenities. And Lily was beginning to think they might just be worth it.

But the question remained—where was she supposed to sleep?

Nigel watched Lillian as she prowled around the suite, investigating the layout. He was afraid she would be disappointed by what she found—namely a single bed in a single bedroom off the main sitting area.

She stood in the doorway, studying the room. He tried to decipher her thought process by her body language—the line of her spine, set of her shoulders, the movements of her hands and fingers dangling at her sides. Unfortunately, she was giving nothing away.

After several long minutes, she turned back around. For a second, she stared at him, looking none too pleased. But then her gaze floated past him and her chest fell as she expelled a breath.

"I guess I can sleep on the sofa," she said, giving him a wide berth as she walked past him. "With luck, maybe it pulls out."

The sofa was long enough for a body to stretch out upon,

but didn't look comfortable enough that anyone would want to. Still, she started removing the cushions one by one, feeling around for a handle that would turn it into her bed for the night.

Nigel opened his mouth to stop her before the first cushion was even taken off, but found himself distracted by the sight of her shapely rear as she leaned over. He'd noticed her change in wardrobe this morning when he'd picked her up for their flight—from the dark, Ashdown Abbey business attire she'd been wearing around the office to a much lighter, brighter dress of unknown origins—but hadn't truly appreciated her current clothing choice until just now.

When she didn't find what she was looking for, she straightened with a huff, putting her hands on her hips. He could have gone on admiring the view all afternoon, but finally took pity on her.

"Nonsense," he said, causing her to spin around, cushions still askew. "There's no need for you to stay on the sofa."

She quirked a brow. "Do you expect me to sleep on the floor, then?"

He gave a snort of laughter. "Certainly not."

The quirked brow lowered as she narrowed both eyes, her mouth flattening into an angry slash. "If you say the bed is big enough for both of us," she all but growled, "I will not be responsible for my actions."

Her frown deepened when he chuckled at her obvious irritation.

"What kind of employer do you think I am?" he couldn't help but tease.

She didn't respond, simply waited, her expression still one of a woman who'd just unwittingly sucked on a lemon.

Crossing the space between them, he cupped her shoulders, giving her an encouraging "buck up" shake before letting his palms slide down her bare arms.

"Surely this suite is spacious enough for the two of us to manage without getting under each other's skin. And we can ask that a cot be brought up before nightfall, set it up out here. I'll use it," he added. "You can stay in the bedroom."

Some of the temper leached out of her features, softening the lines around her mouth and eyes.

"I can't make you do that. This is your suite. You should be able to enjoy the bed."

He had half a mind to inform her that he'd enjoy it best if she joined him there. He hadn't even seen the bed in question yet, but he'd stayed in enough luxury suites to have a pretty good idea of just how expansive and inviting it would be.

Surely enough room for two to sleep comfortably. And more than enough room for them to do much more than that.

Though he knew it was a bad idea all around, he indulged himself for a moment in fantasies of having her naked and in his arms. Of rolling around on slick satin sheets with her. Of having her beneath him, above him, plastered to him by their own perspiration and mutual passion.

His errant thoughts alone caused tiny beads of sweat to break out along his brow and upper lip. He could only imagine the physiological response he might suffer from full-on body-to-body contact of a carnal nature with her.

Which was a problem. A rather large, obvious problem, if she'd cared to glance down and notice as much. Thankfully, she didn't.

But hadn't he sat down just last week and given himself a stern talking-to? Hadn't he learned his lesson with Caroline?

Lessons, plural, he reminded himself now. Thanks to his ill-fated affair with Caroline, he'd learned not to get involved with women who were even loosely involved in the fashion industry, and certainly not one with whom he worked. His own personal assistant would be even worse.

He'd also learned that it was probably wise to avoid any

sort of romantic attachment to American women altogether. Especially when he was trying to get Ashdown Abbey firmly established here in the States. And when his father was breathing down his neck about the delay in that success.

For those reasons and probably hundreds more, Lillian needed to remain off-limits. He couldn't deny that he would enjoy a quick, lusty romp with her. No warm-blooded male could without being accused of lying through his teeth.

But better to lie on a too-short, too-narrow cot in the middle of the sitting room, picturing Lillian on the other side of the bedroom door, than to make one of the biggest mistakes of his life.

No amount of pleasure was worth the destruction crossing that line could bring. Or so he tried to convince himself.

"It's no problem, truly," he told her, wanting to move things away from the hazardous territory his thoughts were treading upon.

Not giving her a chance to protest further, he grabbed her bags and carted them into the other room, setting them at the foot of the bed. When he turned, she was behind him, watching his every move.

"Go ahead and unpack, settle in. I'll call down for a co and ask them to have it delivered by nightfall. In the meantime, I have a business dinner at seven o'clock with the head of one of our most important accounts. I'd like you to come along, if you're feeling up to it."

After a short pause in which she didn't respond, he added, "I'll understand if you're tired from the flight and would prefer to stay in."

"No," she responded quickly, straightening in the doorway. "I'd love to go."

He gave a sharp nod. "Excellent. I'll leave you to freshen up and get ready. We'll leave in an hour, if that's all right."

"Of course."

They both started forward at the same time, she toward her luggage and he toward the bedroom door. Their arms brushed as they passed one another, a jolt of electricity, awareness, summer heat pouring through him. It made him catch his breath, swallow hard and wonder if she was suffering the same disturbing effect…or if he was the only one doomed to spend the weekend drenched in sexual frustrations thicker than the Miami heat.

Eight

Dinner their first night in Miami. Breakfast in the room—but set out so beautifully and served so elegantly that the might as well have been at a five-star restaurant. A business luncheon. And then, the evening before the Saturday morning fashion show, a cocktail party where a handful of those involved in the show—designers, buyers, planners executives—could rub elbows and size up the competition in a friendly, noncompetitive atmosphere.

Lily had known the schedule ahead of time, but hadn't realized how busy or rushed it would actually be.

True to his word, Nigel slept on a cot in the middle of the sitting room of the luxury suite. The roll-away bed looked completely out of place and—to Lily, at least—flashed like a giant neon sign that spelled G-U-I-L-T every time she laid eyes on it.

She didn't have any other ideas or a better solution to their awkward one bed/two bodies predicament, but it still wasn't right that she'd kicked him out of the bedroom of his very own suite.

Guiltiness aside, however, she had to admit she was more than a little relieved to have a door to close and a separate room to escape to each time they returned from yet another business-related outing.

She didn't fear for her safety, exactly—at least not physically. She feared for her sanity and her best intentions.

The longer she was with Nigel, the more she admired him. The more attractive she found him. The more often she caught herself zoning out to simply stare at him, admiring the line of his jaw, the slight bow of his mouth, the way his lips quirked when he was amused or his brows rose when he was curious or intrigued.

What sent her skittering into the bedroom so often under one flimsy excuse or another, though, was the problem she was having regulating her temperature. Oh, how she wished she could blame it on the Florida heat and humidity. Such a nice, handy reason for the hot flashes that kept assailing her at the most inconvenient moments.

But it was hard to point fingers at the weather when the worst of her symptoms seemed to hit mostly indoors, when they were surrounded by comfortable-verging-on-chilly air conditioning.

Which led her to only one terrifying conclusion: it wasn't her current location causing her so many problems…it was Nigel himself.

It was her body, her hormones, her apparently too-long-dormant, ready-to-party-like-it-was-1999 libido kicking up and screaming for attention.

Why couldn't her sex drive have come out of hibernation while she was still in New York? There were men there. Handsome, funny, available men. Or so she'd been led to be-

lieve by her sister, who seemed to find a different one to g
home with every other night.

But seriously, how hard would it have been to—in crud
terms—get laid before flying to Los Angeles, where she wa
pretending to be someone else entirely? Why had she bee
living practically like a nun the past several months, only t
meet Nigel and have her inner pole dancer wake up wantin
to shake her moneymaker?

Oh, yes, she was in trouble. Pretending to be a mild
mannered personal assistant by day, tossing and turning an
fighting the urge to throw open the door and invite Nigel t
join her in the big lonely bed by night.

That was why she made herself scarce at every opportu
nity. That was why she turned the lock on the bedroom doc
each night before she climbed into the king-size bed.

Not to keep him out, but to keep herself in.

But with every tick of the clock, every sleepless hour tha
passed, Lily was losing the battle. The thoughts that spirale
through her head made her hot and restless and frustrated.

Then she would wake up still tired and out of sorts, doin
her best to get her errant emotions under control while sh
dressed and got ready. Thinking she was back to normal an
fully prepared to face Nigel again, she would open the bed
room door…and find him standing there, looking like th
answer to the prayers of single women around the worl
Or he would turn at the sound of the door opening and he
heart would screech to a stop, leaving her chest empty an
her throat burning.

She was amazed she managed to stumble her way throug
the day without doing something truly embarrassing lik
drooling, weeping or collapsing at his feet in a puddle c
needy, pathetic female.

Nigel never showed signs of suspecting her inner turmoi

so she must have been doing a decent job of hiding it. Thank goodness.

Now here she was, holed up once again in the suite bedroom that had caused all of her problems to begin with. And Nigel was out there, once again, waiting for her.

They had time yet before they needed to leave for the pre-show cocktail party, but as cowardly as she knew it was, she couldn't bring herself to spend their in-between time out in the main sitting area.

She'd tried, early on in their stay. They'd talked business, and Nigel had filled her in on what to expect from the weekend and various events they would be attending. But the longer they talked, the more they ran out of things to say, and the more awkward the lengthy pauses became.

Awkward and…tension-filled. As though the air was slowly being sucked out of the room, replaced by a growing electrical current. It would cause her chest to grow tighter by degrees and goose bumps to break out along her skin.

So over and over again, she retreated to the bedroom and relative safety.

She wondered if Nigel was beginning to get suspicious. But even more, she wondered if he felt any of the sizzling awareness, the building attraction that assailed her every time they were alone together.

A part of her hoped he did. After all, she shouldn't be the only one suffering and running for cover like a nervous squirrel.

A bigger part of her, though, hoped that he didn't. Uncontrollable lust and a passionate fling with the man who was supposed to be her boss but was really a possible archnemesis was something she so sincerely didn't need.

It would be much better to suffer in silence, even if her continued run-and-hide routine was becoming increasingly difficult to pull off, while he remained completely oblivious.

At least tonight they would be surrounded by other people
The party would keep them busy, talking and shaking hands
drinking and nibbling on hors d'oeuvres. By the time it wa
all over with and they made their way back to the hotel, the
would both be exhausted and more than ready to go thei
separate ways for a good night's sleep. Or as many hours a
they could squeeze in before having to get up and go to th
fashion show, anyway.

She was walking around in one of the hotel's soft, fluff
terry-cloth robes, fresh from the shower and lining up her un
derthings before beginning to dress, when there was a ligh
tap at the door. Her heart lurched, mouth going dry, becaus
she knew it could only be Nigel.

Swallowing hard, she took a deep breath and tiptoed ove
checking the front of her robe to be sure she wasn't flash
ing too much bare skin before pulling the door open a crack

As expected, Nigel stood on the other side. He was stil
dressed in the clothes he'd been wearing all day, but had re
moved the suit jacket and tie and opened the first few button
of his dress shirt, giving her a rather mouthwatering peek a
the smooth chest beneath.

Through the crack of the door, he looked at her, his gaz
starting at her still-damp hair and skating down the line o
her terry-wrapped body to the tips of her painted toes, the
back up. His eyes glittered as they met hers, sending ripple
of desire to every dark nook and cranny of her being.

Her pulse kicked up and she tried to swallow again, bu
found that both her throat and her lungs refused to function

Thankfully, he saved her from choking on her own word
and sounding like a strangled crow by filling the uncomfor
able silence and speaking first.

"Lillian," he began. "Sorry to disturb you, but I have
small request."

He sounded so serious, she immediately straightened

shifting from vulnerable woman getting dressed to personal assistant on the alert in the blink of an eye.

"Of course," she responded. "What do you need?"

"Would it be too much to ask that you wear something special this evening?"

Her brow rose. Images of lacy teddies and garter belts with silken stockings filled her head. Surely he couldn't mean *that* sort of "special."

From out of nowhere, around the other side of the door-jamb, he revealed a long, hunter green garment bag with the Ashdown Abbey logo embroidered in the upper right-hand corner.

"This is one of the gowns from the line we'll be showing tomorrow. I was hoping I could talk you into wearing it to-night as a bit of a sneak peek for our competition."

He shot her a lopsided grin, accompanied by a wicked wink, and she couldn't help smiling in return.

"I'll be happy to try," she told him, reaching toward the top of the garment bag where he held it by a thick, satin-wrapped hanger. "But I'm not exactly a supermodel. It may not fit."

His gaze flitted down her fluffy white form once again, as though he could see straight through the robe to the body beneath.

"I think you'll be fine. We don't design for stick-thin women to begin with, even when it comes to runway shows, and this dress in particular is a very accommodating design."

"All right," she said with a small nod.

She'd brought one of her own elegant maxi dresses with her that would have been perfectly acceptable for a cocktail party, but she had to admit she was curious to see what Nigel wanted her to wear. And it was more than a little flattering to be asked to model one of Ashdown Abbey's brand-new, as-yet-unseen designs in front of other designers and associ-ates for the first time.

She would rather be showing off her *own* creations, of course, but since she wouldn't be able to reveal that they were her designs, anyway…well, beggars couldn't be choosers.

Still standing there, dress in hand, bedroom door open, she wasn't quite sure what else to say. It didn't seem right to simply slam the door in Nigel's face, even though she was eager to peel open the garment bag and see what lay inside.

Finally, he said, "I'll give you a few minutes. Let me know if you have any problems."

With that, he took a step back, but seemed reluctant to move away. And she was equally reluctant to close the door, shutting herself in again. But they did have a party to get to.

"I'll only be a few minutes," she murmured.

"Take your time. The limo won't be here to pick us up for an hour yet."

She disappeared back inside her luxurious little Girl Cave as he turned and headed off to get ready himself. Hanging the garment bag on the open armoire door, she slid the center zipper all the way down and peeled back the sides.

It was almost like scratching a lottery ticket. She held her breath, slowly revealing the gown beneath.

As lottery tickets *and* designer gowns went, it was a winner. Stunning. Gorgeous. Awe-inspiring. And for her, just a bit envy inducing.

The sheer, champagne-colored chiffon shimmered in the light and with every movement, no matter how slight.

The ruched bodice ran at an angle to the single beaded shoulder strap, about two inches wide, leaving the other shoulder entirely bare. A wide swath of the same jewels from the shoulder made up a belted waistline of sorts.

From the waist down, the chiffon flowed in angled layers over the same-colored charmeuse all the way to what she assumed would be the floor once she put it on.

Suddenly, she was both excited and nervous at the prospect of modeling it. Not surprisingly, the dress was beautiful. But she hadn't worn anything this fancy in a very, very long time. And now, not only was she being asked to dress up like she was attending a royal wedding, but she would be expected to "sell" another designer's work.

Knowing she didn't have a choice, she hurried back to the bathroom to finish with her hair and makeup, then returned to the main room and shrugged out of the terry-cloth robe. Even though she'd planned for a cocktail party and packed accordingly, the underthings she'd brought didn't quite suit the gown she would now be wearing.

If Nigel had shown her the dress ahead of time, she probably would have taken a quick shopping trip for something a bit sexier. Stockings instead of nylons, perhaps, and a bra and panty set the same color as the gown.

Luckily, some of the bras and panties she had with her were pale enough not to be seen through the champagne material. And though the bra wasn't strapless, the straps were able to be rearranged or removed completely. She would just have to hope it stayed up and in place all night.

Moments later, she was reaching for the gown, turning it around and searching for the narrow hidden zipper that ran the length of the back. Time to see if the design was as forgiving as Nigel claimed.

Stepping into the pool of material, she drew it up and slipped the single strap over her left shoulder. The bodice settled over her breasts and the cups of her bra, the rest of the gown falling into place from her midriff down.

Reaching around, she clutched the two sides of the dress at the back in one hand and held them together. The fit might be snug, but she thought it would work. Especially if she held her stomach in most of the time.

She looked okay, too, judging by her reflection in the bureau mirror. Provided the dress stayed in one piece once she got it zipped up. Which she couldn't quite manage on her own.

Butterflies unfurling at the base of her belly, she moved to the bedroom door and opened it, slowly and quietly. Venturing into the other room, she glanced around, searching for Nigel. She might not *want* to ask for his help, but she kind of needed it.

But the sitting room was empty.

Still holding the gown closed behind her with one hand, she strolled farther into the room, checking the balcony and wondering if he'd left the suite entirely for some reason.

Then she heard a click and turned just as he stepped out of the guest bath looking like a million bucks. Maybe one point eight.

He was wearing a tuxedo. Just a plain black tuxedo, the same as men had been wearing for decades.

And yet Lily would be willing to bet he looked better in it than any other man in the history of tuxedos. The word *scrumptious* came to mind. As well as *delectable* and—as Zoe might say—*hunkalicious*.

The midnight-black jacket and slacks fit him like a glove. If they hadn't been tailored specifically for him, it was the finest bit of off-the-rack sewing she'd ever seen.

His sandy-brown hair was combed back, slightly wavy but every strand in place.

And the tie at his throat…well, there was something about that tight, classic bow and the gold cuff links at his wrists that made her want to drop her arm, let the gown drop to the floor, and stalk forward to start peeling him out of his own uptight party wear.

The thought stopped her cold. Made her give herself a mental shake and stern reminder that lusting after the boss was a bad, bad idea.

Of course, on the heels of that came the notion that she

wouldn't mind being a bad girl. Just for a little while. And only with Nigel.

His mind may have been wandering down the same wicked path, because his eyes snapped with flecks of green fire the minute he saw her. His gaze raked her from head to toe, and she could have sworn a tiny muscle flexed along his jaw.

She drew a deep breath, which caused the bodice of the not-yet-zipped dress to slide down a notch. Pinning it in place with her only remaining free hand, she cleared her throat and smiled weakly.

"I need a little help," she murmured.

He raised a brow, his attention still glued to her lower-than-intended décolletage.

By way of explanation, she turned, giving him her back and showing the long, open rear of the gown.

She felt rather than saw him move behind her and grasp the small tab of the zipper near the base of her spine. In a slow, gentle glide, he pulled it up.

When it was high enough, she dropped the arm that had been holding the two sides together and moved it instead to her nape, where she brushed aside her loose hair. The back of the dress only reached her shoulder blades, but better safe than sorry.

As he reached the top of the zipper, his knuckles brushed her bare skin, sending shivers rippling across her body in every direction. She braced herself and tried not to let that shiver show, but she felt it all the way to her toes.

Long seconds ticked by while she stood unmoving, not blinking, not even daring to breathe. And then Nigel stepped back, his hands falling away from her bare flesh.

Relief washed through her…but so did regret.

"There," he said, the single word coming out somewhat gruff.

Lily let go of her hair and turned again to face him. This time, his gaze seemed to be taking in the detail of the gown.

"Lovely," he told her with a nod of approval. "As I knew it would be."

Lifting his eyes to hers, he asked, "What do you think?"

"It's beautiful," she answered honestly, smoothing a hand over the front of the dress and then fluffing it a bit to show the ethereal layering of the skirt. It flowed and fell like angels' wings, almost as though it wasn't there at all.

"And how does it feel?" Nigel wanted to know. "Comfortable enough to wear for the evening?"

"I think so," she told him. It was rather nice of him to ask. Most employers—most men, for that matter—wouldn't bother.

"I'll need to find some jewelry and shoes that go with the dress," she added, "but it fits better than I would have expected."

"Ah," he said, holding up his index finger and offering a crooked grin. "I believe I can help with that."

Leading her over to the sofa in the middle of the room, he began opening boxes that had been stacked across its narrow length and pulling out bits of tissue paper from around whatever the boxes held.

"I had them send over some of the footwear for tomorrow's show. All of the shoes for the line are similar in style and we always make sure to have extras on hand, but I wasn't sure of your size."

He stepped back, gesturing for her to take a look, pick out whatever she needed. Brushing past him in her bare feet, she peeked and found an array of gorgeous, very expensive footwear.

They were, indeed, all very similar, making her even more curious to see the entire line. She wanted to know what de signs Ashdown Abbey had created to go with all of these shoes…or vice versa, actually.

Checking sizes, she chose a pair of strappy gold open-toed heels and balanced on the arm of the sofa to slip them on. Even before she stood up again and glanced down to see how they looked with the dress and her painted nails peeping out, she knew they would be perfect with the gown.

Lifting her head, she found Nigel's eyes on her. Intense. Blazing. The air caught in her lungs and refused to budge.

Seconds ticked by, then minutes. Finally, he cleared his throat and reached for something else amidst the boxes and loose tissue paper.

"This should complete the look nicely," he said, flipping open the lid of a large, flat, velvet-lined box.

Inside was a breathtaking necklace and earring set. Champagne diamonds in exquisite gold settings. And if they were real—which something told her they were—they had to be worth a small fortune.

Plucking the earrings from their bed of black velvet, he dropped them into her palm. Then he removed the necklace and stepped around her to stand at her back.

Lifting the sweep of loose, wavy curls she'd worked so hard on, she waited for him to finish with the fastener before dropping her hair and pressing her fingers to her throat to touch and straighten the main pendant and surrounding web of gems.

"This is a lot of expensive fashion. Are you sure you trust me to wear it out of the suite?" she asked somewhat shakily, only half teasing.

"You aren't planning to run off with it all at the stroke of midnight, are you? Like Cinderella," he teased in return.

She certainly felt like Cinderella. A young woman pretending to be someone other than who she really was, dressed to the nines to attend a grand ball with a man who definitely qualified as a Prince Charming.

She only hoped her true identity didn't become known as the clock struck midnight, as he said. That might possibly be worse than running off with thousands, maybe hundreds of thousands of dollars' worth of Ashdown Abbey property.

Since she had no intention of doing the latter, she knew she was safe on that count. It was the former she needed to worry about. But with luck, it wouldn't be an issue tonight or at any time on this trip.

She hoped not once they returned to Los Angeles, either, but one thing at a time. First she needed to get through this evening. Then tomorrow's fashion show…then the remainder of their short stay in Miami…then their return to Los Angeles… She would deal with the rest after that.

"I'm no Cinderella," she said by way of answer.

"No," Nigel responded.

The single word came out short and clipped, drawing her attention to his face and the hard glint of his hazel eyes.

"Cinderella could never look so lovely in this gown or these jewels," he added more softly.

Lily's heart stuttered in her chest. Okay, that was definitely more than a simple compliment. That was…a come-on. A warning. A promise of things to come.

She knew now, without a shadow of a doubt, that Nigel felt at least a fraction of the attraction to her that she felt toward him. The lust she'd been feeling, the shocks of static electricity whenever they were in the same room together, were *not* one-sided.

Which was good. It was nice to know she wasn't going crazy or nursing an awkward schoolgirl crush on the captain of the football team whom she would never in a million years have a shot with.

But it was bad, too. Because while she might be able to

keep a lid on her own out-of-control emotions and baser in-
stincts, she couldn't be sure that lid wouldn't come flying off
in the face of his pent-up passions if he decided to point them
in her direction and throw caution to the wind.

Already her mouth was growing dry, her hands damp. Her
pulse had kicked up to a near-arrhythmia pace. And every
other portion of her body was heating at an alarming rate,
sending a flush of inappropriate longing across her face and
her upper body.

If Nigel noticed her state of distress, he didn't comment.
Instead, he held an arm out, offering his elbow.

"Shall we?"

Saved by the RSVP and waiting limousine, she thought,
releasing a small, relieved breath.

"Yes, thank you," she replied, wrapping her hand around
his firm forearm.

They glided to the door so smoothly their movements
might have been choreographed. If they could keep up such
astounding synchronicity, Lily thought they might, just *might,*
be able to pull this off.

Not only her pretense of being someone she wasn't, but of
hiding the sexual tension that—to her mind, at least—rolled
off the pair of them in waves.

But while the outside world was likely to see merely a
very handsome, rich and successful businessman escorting
his fair-to-middling female assistant to an industry function,
she was almost painfully conscious of the heat from Nigel's
body burning through the fabric of his tuxedo jacket to all
but scorch her fingertips. Of the rapid beat of her heart behind the bodice of her borrowed gown. Of every second that
ticked by when she could think of nothing but being alone
with Nigel in a very naked, nonprofessional capacity.

Nine

Hours later, the noise and crowd of the cocktail party behind them, Lily sat beside Nigel in the rear of the limo as it carried them back to the Royal Crown. Her eyes were closed, her head resting against the plush leather seat. To say she was tired would be a tremendous understatement.

As though reading her mind, Nigel's knuckles brushed her cheek, tucking a strand of hair behind her ear.

"Tired?" he asked.

His touch was featherlight and possibly one-hundred percent innocent, but still it had her sucking in a breath and fighting to maintain her equilibrium.

Rolling her head to the side, she forced her eyes open, braced for the impact of meeting his gaze. It still hit her like a steamroller.

Knowing she wouldn't be able to form coherent words to respond to his query, she merely nodded.

One corner of his mouth tipped up in an understanding

smile. "You were incredible tonight," he told her in a soft voice that washed over her like warm honey.

"You look amazing," he continued. "Better than any model we could have hired to showcase this design. And the way you are with people…you're a natural. You had everyone at the party eating out of your hand. The men especially. Well, the straight ones, at any rate," he added with a teasing wink.

Despite her weariness, she couldn't help but return his grin of amusement. "I'm glad you approve. I don't mind telling you I was nervous about tonight. I didn't want to embarrass you *or* do anything in this beautiful gown to put a damper on tomorrow's show."

"Not possible," he said with a sharp shake of his head. "You were…extraordinary. As I knew you would be."

His heartfelt compliment made her blush and filled her with unexpected pleasure. She shouldn't be happy that he was so impressed with her performance tonight. She should be annoyed. Sorry that she'd helped to bolster his or Ashdown Abbey's reputation in any way.

But she *was* pleased. Both that she'd maintained her ruse as a personal assistant, and that she'd done well enough to earn Nigel's praise.

She was candid enough with herself to admit that the last didn't have as much to do with his standing as her "boss" as with him as a man.

"Thank you," she murmured, her throat surprisingly tight and slightly raw.

"No," he replied, once again brushing the back of his hand along her cheek. "Thank *you*."

And then, before she realized what he was about to do, he leaned in, pressing his mouth to hers.

For a moment, she remained lax, too stunned to move or respond. But his lips were so soft and inviting, and she'd been imagining what it would be like to kiss him for so long…

With a low mewl of longing, she shifted into his arms, bringing her own up to grasp his shoulders. She opened to him, letting her lips part, her body melt against his and everything in her turn liquid.

Nigel groaned, pulling her to him with even more force, his wide palm cupping the base of her spine while his tongue traced the line of her mouth, then delved inside at her clear invitation.

The world fell away while they ate at each other, devoured each other, groped each other like a couple of randy teenagers.

A million reasons why they shouldn't be doing this clamored through her head. But those doubts and fears were little more than a low-level hum behind the loud roar of desire, yearning, need.

Despite the regrets she might suffer later, right now she didn't care. She couldn't remember ever being kissed this way, ever wanting a man as much as she wanted Nigel Statham.

He was danger and sex and exotic intrigue on two legs, with a bone-tingling British accent to boot. How women didn't adhere themselves to him like dryer lint throughout the day she didn't know.

How amazing was it, then, that he seemed to be attracted to her? Seemed to want her?

Maybe he put the moves on all of his personal assistants. Maybe one of his goals while he was in the United States was to shag, as he might say, as many American girls as possible.

If that was the case, she expected to be really annoyed later on. At the moment, however, she was more than willing to be just another notch on this handsome Brit's bedpost.

While one hand kneaded the small of her back, his other swept up to the bodice of the couture gown, cupping her breast, stroking through the material. Despite the thick ruching and bra beneath, her nipples beaded, drawing a moan of desire from deep in her throat.

Nigel answered with a groan of his own, increasing the pressure of his mouth against her lips. There was barely a breath of air between them, but even that was too much. And as he thrust his tongue around hers over and over, she met him with equal ferocity, sucking, licking, drinking him in.

He smelled of the most wonderful cologne. Something fresh and clean, with a hint of spice. Whatever the brand, she was sure it was expensive. And worth every penny, since it made her want to lick him from clavicle to calf, inhale him in one shuddering gulp, absorb him into her own skin like sunshine on a warm summer day.

But if he smelled good, he tasted even better. Warm and rich, like the wine he'd been sipping all evening at the party, with a hint of the whiskey he'd downed toward the end. She didn't even particularly care for whiskey, but if it meant drinking it from his lips and the tip of his tongue, she could easily drown in the stuff on a regular basis.

Nigel's hand was trailing down her side, sweeping the curve of her breast, her waist, her hip and slowly inching the long skirt of the dress upward when the limousine came to a smooth but noticeable halt. A second later, the driver's side door opened and Nigel pulled back with a fiercely muttered, "Bollocks."

Quickly, before the fog of passion had even begun to clear from her brain, he straightened her gown and the lines of his own tuxedo, taking a moment to swipe lipstick from both her mouth and his just as the lock on the rear door of the limo clicked.

By the time the door swung all the way open to reveal the driver standing there waiting for them, everything looked completely normal. Professional, even. Nigel and Lily were sitting at least a foot apart, canted away from each other on the wide bench seat, as though they hadn't even been speaking, let alone groping one another like horny octopi.

Without a word, Nigel exited the car, then helped her out.

Nigel thanked the driver, passed him a generous tip and escorted Lily into the main entrance of the hotel. They passed through the lobby, her heels clicking on the marble floor until they reached the elevators. Inside, they were silent, facing the doors and standing inches apart, even though they were alone in the confined space.

When they reached their floor, Nigel gestured for her to step out ahead of him, then took her elbow as they moved quietly down the carpeted hallway. The perfect gentleman. The perfectly polite employer with no lascivious thoughts whatsoever about the assistant who was staying in his suite with him.

With some distance now from that amazing kiss in the limousine, Lily wasn't sure what to think or how to feel.

Did she want to pick up where they'd left off as soon as they got into the suite? A shiver assaulted her at the very thought.

Or did she want to put the kiss behind her? Chalk it up to the heat of the moment and go their separate ways once they got inside? That thought made her a little sad, which surprised her.

Reaching the door, she waited for Nigel to slide the key card through the lock and decided to play it by ear.

If he began to ravish her the minute the door closed behind them, she would go limp and let it happen. No doubt enjoying every step of the way.

If he returned to his usual quiet and respectfully reserved self, not coming anywhere near her again…she would do the same. It might even be for the best, regardless of how much she would mourn the loss of his lips, the taste of him on the tip of her tongue.

As she entered the suite ahead of him, her heartbeat picked up, the tempo echoing in her ears as her anticipation grew. But he didn't grab her the second the door closed behind them, didn't push her against the wall and begin the ravishment she'd been fantasizing about. They stepped into the sitting room. Perfectly polite. Perfectly civilized.

The sound of Nigel clearing his throat made her jump. She turned slowly to face him, disappointed when she didn't find him stalking toward her, desire burning in his hazel-green eyes.

"I feel as though I should apologize for what happened in the car," he murmured in a low, slow tone of voice.

Her heart plummeted. Well, she supposed that answered the question of what he thought about the kiss, didn't it? She tried not to be offended—hadn't she already admitted to herself that fooling around with her boss-slash-possible enemy was a bad idea?—but couldn't help being slightly hurt. After all, to her, the kiss had been one step away from spontaneous combustion.

"But quite frankly," he continued when she didn't respond, "I'm not that sorry."

Her eyes widened, locking with his. What she saw there was the same passion she'd experienced in the limo. The same need, the same longing…but banked to a slow burn rather than a blazing inferno.

"Which makes what I have to ask next rather awkward."

Lily swallowed, the blood in her veins going thick and hot.

"Would you mind stepping out of your gown?"

She blinked. That wasn't so bad. A little odd, yes, but only because she would have expected him to be closer when he made the request. Maybe whisper it in her ear or want to strip it from her body himself.

But if watching her disrobe was part of his fantasy, she could certainly comply.

And then he went and ruined whatever small thread of fantasy had been forming in *her* head.

"The dress and shoes need to be returned before tomorrow's show."

"Oh." Yes, of course. The fashion show. She was walking around in one of its borrowed designs.

"Sure," she said, fumbling for both words and clear thoughts. "Just…give me a minute."

Feeling unsure and uncoordinated, she turned toward the bedroom and crossed the distance with as much dignity as she could muster while kicking herself for being seven kinds of fool.

Closing the door behind her, she moved robotically, removing the necklace, earrings, bracelet and ring, and setting them on top of the bureau. Then she toed off the strappy ice-pick heels. And though she nearly dislocated her shoulder doing it, she managed to grasp the tab of the gown's zipper at her back and tug it all the way down. Stepping out of the dress, she returned it to its satin hanger inside the garment bag, then zipped that closed.

Since she couldn't go back out to the rest of the suite in her underwear, she covered herself with the same fluffy hotel robe as earlier, which she'd left lying at the foot of the bed.

Gathering all of Nigel's borrowed items, she strode back into the sitting room. He was standing exactly where she'd left him, but she refused to meet his gaze. She'd had quite enough humiliation and emotional up-and-down, back-and-forth for one night, thank you very much.

Walking to the sofa, she draped the garment bag over the arm, dropped the shoes back in their tissue-paper-lined box, and laid the collection of pricey jewelry on the low coffee table.

"There you go," she told him, her tone clipped, even to her own ears. And still she wouldn't look at him. "Thank you again for letting me wear them tonight. It was a privilege."

Truth. It *had* been a privilege…right up until the moment it became pain.

With that, she turned and marched back to the bedroom, spine straight, head held high. She remained that way until after she'd closed and locked the door. Until she'd shed the robe and her underthings, leaving them in a pile on the bathroom floor. Until she'd stepped into the hot spray of the shower, letting the sharp beads of water pummel her, pound her, drown her in mindless sensation.

Only then did she let go of her rigid control, let oxygen back into her lungs and the hurt into her soul.

Only then did she crumble.

Well, that didn't go quite as he'd planned. And he felt like a total prat.

The kiss in the limousine had been anything but forgettable. There had been moments when he'd thought he might implode from the sensations that assailed him at the mere touch of Lillian's lips against his own.

It had taken every ounce of self-control he possessed to pull away from her when the car stopped, and to get them both set to rights before their driver came around to open his door and got more than an eyeful. Thank goodness he'd retained enough of his senses to even notice the slowing of the vehicle.

The walk into the hotel and ride up in the lift had been another agonizing test of his control. He'd wanted nothing more than to turn on her once the doors slid closed, press her up against the wall, and continue from where they'd left off. Kissing, caressing, fogging the glass…or in this case, the mirrored walls.

Every step down the narrow pathway to their suite, he'd imagined what he would do to her as soon as they were shut safely inside. Alone and away from prying eyes.

But he couldn't very well pounce on her the minute the

door swung shut, could he? She might have thought him a sex-crazed maniac. Or worse, believed that whether or not she acquiesced might impact her job.

Nigel muttered a colorful oath. The *last* thing he needed was a sexual-harassment complaint brought against him or the company.

But more than that, he didn't want to be *that* fellow—the one who flirted with his secretary, made her believe that there might be recompense if she went along with his advances… and the unemployment line if she didn't.

And he *never* wanted Lillian to think that of him. Professional status and reputation be damned. His attraction to her was genuine—if ill conceived—and he wanted her to know that. He wanted her to be genuinely attracted to him, as well. Where was the fun in any of this if she wasn't?

He'd thought he was being witty and smooth by asking her to remove the dress for tomorrow's show. True, he did need to get it back so that it would be ready and waiting for its respective model by morning.

Inside his addled and obviously not very intelligent mind, however, he'd imagined her slinking out of the dress and shoes—either right there in front of him or in the privacy of the bedroom—and then him suavely murmuring that *now that she was naked, how would she feel about picking up where they'd left off?*

It had all sounded so bloody brilliant as he'd played it out over and over in his head. And then somehow he'd mucked it up. He'd said the wrong thing or said it the wrong way.

Something had gone cockeyed, because Lillian's face had transformed from soft and mistily content to shocked and hurt.

He'd missed the chance to apologize and set the matter straight before she disappeared into the bedroom. Then when she'd come out, he'd been too gobsmacked and tongue-tied by his own stupidity to rectify the situation before she ran off again.

Bloody hell. What was it about this woman that turned him into a complete wanker?

Regardless, he had to fix it. He might not be spending the rest of the evening exactly as he'd hoped—naked and writhing around with Lillian on that king-size bed he had yet to sleep in—but he couldn't let her storm off thinking he was a git. That the kiss they'd shared meant nothing or that getting Ashdown Abbey's dress back safe and sound was more important to him than what was blooming to life between them.

Long minutes passed while he tried to decide how to go about cleaning up the mess he'd made. The clock on the mantel counted them down, grating on his nerves even as he paced in time with the steady *tick-tick-tick* of the second hand going round.

After wearing a path in front of the sofa, he moved closer to the bedroom door. He could hear the faint sound of water running and assumed she was taking a shower.

The thought of her stripped bare, standing beneath the steaming jets, made it increasingly hard to concentrate. It made other things hard, as well. Especially when he pictured her working up a lather of soap and rubbing it all along her body. Stroking, smoothing, scrubbing. First her arms, then her breasts and torso and…lower.

A thin line of perspiration broke out along his upper lip and his muscles went tense. He'd never known that the act of getting clean could be so dirty. And he very much wanted to walk in there to assist with both.

Chances were he'd get his face slapped for his trouble. He had to *talk* to her first. Work on seducing her back into the shower second.

The water shut off suddenly. And he strained to listen for

movement on the other side of the door while bracing himself with both hands against the jamb on this one.

He didn't want to frighten her, and chances were he was the last person she wanted to see right now, but he needed to talk to her.

Waiting a few minutes until he thought she would be finished in the bathroom but not yet climbing into bed, he tapped lightly on the door.

His palms were damp. His chest was actually tight with anxiety.

This wasn't like him at all. He hadn't been riddled with nerves about facing a girl since… Had he ever been? At university he'd even been a bit of a ladies' man, if he said so himself.

And now he was sweating like David Beckham after a particularly rigorous football match at just the prospect of confronting Lillian once again. Especially when he knew it would mostly involve groveling and apologizing and begging her not to continue believing he was a total squit.

When long moments passed without her opening the door, he began to suspect she was avoiding him. Not that he blamed her. But he knew she was in there, knew she'd heard his knock and knew she couldn't possibly be asleep yet.

He cocked a brow. Well, now he was growing somewhat annoyed.

He knocked again, louder this time. If need be, he would go in there with or without her invitation—after all, it was his suite, and he'd been generous up to now allowing her to have the spacious bedroom and master bath all to herself. Though he'd much prefer she open the door voluntarily so he wouldn't have to add overbearing bullying to his list of crimes tonight.

Just when he was about to try the door himself, he heard a small snick and the knob began to turn. The door opened only a crack, the light from the sitting room illuminating

ust one eye and a narrow portion of Lillian's face. The rest
was left in shadow by the darkness of the bedroom beyond.

"Yes?"

Her voice was low, flat and far from friendly when she
said it.

"I'm sorry to disturb you," he began.

Which was so very close to simply *I'm sorry,* yet he managed to skirt a straight-out apology. Brilliant.

"Could I speak to you for a moment?" he tried again, still
taking the coward's way out.

"It's late," she told him, keeping the door open no more
than a single inch. "I'm tired. We can talk in the morning."

And with that, she closed the door. Soundly, firmly and
with a clicking lock of finality.

Bugger. Nigel barely resisted the urge to smack his fist
against the solid door frame.

Well, he'd mucked that up good and proper, hadn't he?
Damn it all. The bloody dress that had started this debacle
was on its way back to join the rest of the collection and await
tomorrow's fashion show, while he was still trying to find a
way to mop up the mess he'd made.

He took a deep breath, as frustrated with Lillian's refusal
to speak to him as with his own bungled efforts.

Enough of this. It was going to be dealt with right here,
right now and that was the end of it.

Raising his hand, he knocked again, hard enough that she
couldn't help but hear the summons and know he meant business.

"Go away, Mr. Statham."

Oh, so it was back to Mr. Statham, was it? When she'd just
begun to call him Nigel.

There was only one thing to be done about that.

Leaning close to the door, he lowered his voice and ordered, "Open this door, Lillian."

He could have sworn he heard a snort of derision, followed by a mumbled, "I don't think so."

His jaw locked, teeth grinding together until he thought they might snap.

Slowly, carefully, enunciating every word, he bit out "Open this door, Lillian, right now."

He paused, listening for movement, but heard none. "You have until the count of three," he told her, sounding like every angry father in every movie he'd ever seen, "or I'll kick it in."

In truth, he wasn't certain he *could* kick the door in. He prided himself on staying in shape, playing at least a game or two of squash per week, in addition to his regular exercise routine. But nothing in his past led him to believe he would have either the strength or the martial-arts-like coordination necessary to actually break down a door.

And then there was the sturdiness of the door itself. Not to mention the lock, which—hotel quality or not—might just prove to be un-break-down-able. He rather hoped he didn't have to find out.

Stepping backward, he took a deep breath, steeled himself, and got ready to follow through on his promise.

And then there came a click. And the muted turn of the knob.

He watched as the brass-plated handle inched around, letting the air seep from his lungs on a slow exhale and the tension leach from his tendons.

Once again, she opened the door only a crack, but at least this time it was a couple of inches instead of only one. Popping her head out, dark blond hair still damp from her shower, she glared at him.

"Are you threatening me?" she asked, eyes crackling like lapis. "Because that smacks of a threat. Or possibly even harassment. I've got a phone in here with 9-1-1 on speed dial, and I'm not afraid to use it."

Nigel sighed, resisting the urge to rub a hand over his face in frustration. With her. With himself.

"Just a moment of your time," he said. "Please."

When she didn't immediately slam the door in his face, he soldiered on.

"I wanted to apologize for earlier."

Her lashes fluttered as she narrowed her eyes a pinch, but he ignored the warning. With luck she would hear him out and stop shooting daggers.

"It wasn't my intention to offend you by asking you to remove the dress so it could be returned for the show tomorrow. In retrospect, I might have worded my request a bit differently."

He watched her arch a brow, her grip on the edge of the door loosening slightly. She even let it drift open another fraction of an inch.

"For instance, I should have said that the sooner we got the dress off you and headed back for the show, the sooner we could return to what we were doing in the car. Or better yet, I should have ripped the dress off you as soon as we stepped into the suite and said to hell with the show. So we'd be short a look and a model would be sent home in tears…it would have been worth it to avoid hurting your feelings, as I obviously did. And to be making love to you right now instead of standing here having this conversation, hoping you won't slam the door in my face. Again."

There, he'd said it. It had pained him, especially in the region of his pride, which seemed to currently be residing near his solar plexus, making it feel as though a very heavy anvil were pressing down on his diaphragm.

Now to see if it had any impact on Lillian whatsoever, or if she would, indeed, slam the door in his face for a second time. He watched her carefully, trying to judge her response from the one eye, one cheek and half of her mouth that were visible.

Her lashes fluttered, and her tongue darted out to lick those lips nervously.

And then the door began to creak open—so slowly, he thought he might be imagining things.

But the door did open, all the way. And she stepped out into the light of the sitting room. Behind her, he could see that one of the lamps beside the king-size bed was lit, but it wasn't bright enough to fill the entire room.

She was wearing one of the hotel robes, covered from neck to ankle by thick, white terry cloth. She should have looked shapeless and unattractive, but instead she looked adorable. Her hair hung past her shoulders in damp, wavy strands, her flesh pink from its recent scrubbing.

With the belt pulled tight, he could easily make out her feminine curves. The flare of her hips, the dip of her waist, the swell of her breasts. A V of skin and very slight shadow of cleavage were visible in the open neckline of the robe, making him want to linger, stare, nudge the soft lapels apart to reveal even more.

He was on extremely thin ice with her already, however, and didn't think it wise to press his luck. No matter how loudly his libido might be clamoring for him to do just that...and more.

Threading her arms across her chest, she watched him warily.

"So you don't...regret what happened in the limo?" she asked quietly.

Nigel's heart gave a thump of encouragement. If she was asking, that meant she'd been thinking about it. Thinking and worrying.

Taking a cautious step forward, he flexed his fingers to keep from reaching for her. But he answered clearly, honestly, consequences be damned.

"Not even if you call the authorities, as you threatened

Or file a sexual-harassment complaint at Ashdown Abbey, as you have every right to do."

She seemed to consider that for a moment, and then the stiffness began to disappear from her rigid stance. Her expression lightened, her arms loosening to drop to her sides.

Taking a deep breath that lifted the front of the robe in a way that shouldn't have been seductive but was, she let it out on a long sigh.

"This is a bad idea," she murmured, letting her gaze skitter to the side so that he wasn't certain if she was speaking to him or more to herself.

"I'm working for you," she continued. "You could fire me or use me because I'm in your employ. Things could get ugly."

Nigel's shoulders fell almost imperceptibly, and he felt as though his entire bone structure slumped inside his skin. She was right, of course, but that wasn't at all the reaction he'd been hoping for.

"True," he acquiesced, albeit grudgingly. "Though I'm *not* using you, and I would never fire you over something… personal. Something that I would be equally responsible for and took equal part in."

Her eyes locked on his. "You're that noble, are you?"

His chin went up, every ounce of the pride and dignity driven into him from birth coming to the fore. "Yes. I am."

It was her turn to slump as she let out a breath. "I was afraid of that," she said, sounding almost resigned.

And then her voice dropped, but he had no trouble hearing her. No trouble making out both the words and the meaning.

"I'm not sorry, either. About what happened in the limo."

Ten

Lily knew she *should* be sorry about what had happened in the limo. She should also have graciously accepted Nigel's apology without saying anything more, then turned and locked herself back in the bedroom.

Oh, how smart that would have been.

Oh, how she wished she had that much strength of will.

But no matter how hurt and offended she'd been by Nigel's actions concerning the dress, she hadn't been able to stop thinking about *that kiss* the entire time she'd been in the shower. Even through her tears and ragged breathing, her body had hummed with unspent passion. With need and longing and plain old *want*.

Her thoughts had swirled with *what-if*s. What if they hadn't been interrupted by their arrival at the hotel? What if she hadn't been wearing one of the designs for tomorrow's fashion show? What if he'd kissed her in the elevator, then pounced on her like a cat on a mouse the minute they'd reached the room?

What if everything from the past forty minutes had happened far differently and they were in bed right now? Making love. Exploring each other to their hearts' content. Scratching the itch that had plagued her since the first moment she'd met him.

She shouldn't want any of that. She should be smart enough or even angry enough at his possible involvement in the theft of her designs to slam the door on all of it. To man up and stop letting her hormones do her thinking for her.

But she couldn't. Or at least none of her attempts so far had been successful.

So she was giving up. If you couldn't beat 'em, join 'em, right?

She knew now that Nigel was just as attracted to her as she was to him. That what she'd felt in the limo when they kissed hadn't been one-sided. And she just wanted to throw caution to the wind, to be with a man who made her toes curl and her insides feel like molten lava.

And so what if she did? Nigel didn't know who she really was, and she wasn't going to be around that much longer. A few weeks, maybe a month more. Just until she solved her mystery and could return home with information that would save and vindicate her company.

Nigel never even needed to know her true identity. She'd done a fairly good job as his personal assistant so far, if she did say so herself. And knowing it wasn't permanent employment, that he wasn't going to be her boss forever, made it even easier to justify a hot, steamy fling. She could let her hair down, have a good time, and walk away with no consequences. With a quick letter of resignation and excuse about getting another job elsewhere—preferably far away, but without hinting at her true residence in New York—she could wipe the slate clean.

So this was almost like a freebie. Casual, no-strings vacation sex.

Considering how long it had been for her, how long since she'd had a date or sex—casual or otherwise—all she could think was *yes, please*.

Which was why she'd come clean and told him that she didn't regret what had taken place between them after the party, either. She'd wanted him to tear her dress off her body and take her up against the nearest wall of the suite the minute they'd set foot inside.

Well, maybe not that dress, but *a* dress.

And she didn't want to spend the rest of the night alone in that immense bed, tossing and turning and unfulfilled.

Watching his eyes go dark and glinting at her softly spoken admission, she took a deep breath and decided to press on, letting him know in no uncertain terms *exactly* what she meant.

"As much as I enjoyed modeling one of Ashdown Abbey's newest designs, I wish I hadn't been wearing that dress tonight. Because I would have enjoyed having you rip my clothes off the second we walked through the door."

His eyes darkened even more, his jaw tightening until a muscle ticked near his ear.

"Be very certain of what you're saying, Lillian," he grated, the words sounding as though they were being dragged from the depths of his soul. "Because once we begin, there will be no stopping. No more noble gentleman. No more polite facade."

Shivers rocked her nerve endings at what he left unspoken. That once they stopped dancing around their need for each other, once they dropped all pretenses and got down to business, it would be raw, primal, unapologetic S-E-X.

Swallowing hard, she took a single step forward. Determined. Ready.

"I understand," she told him. "And I'm not slamming the door in your face."

Heat exploded across Nigel's face. Lighting up his eyes like emeralds, rolling off his body in waves and battering her like a storm front.

He closed the distance between them without a word, moving in almost a blur of motion. One minute he was over there, the next he was grabbing her by the arms and yanking her to him with such force, her feet nearly left the ground.

His mouth crashed down on hers, twining, mating, devouring. She met him kiss for kiss, thrust for thrust.

He tasted just as he had in the limo—only better, because this time she knew it wasn't a one-time-only, heat-of-the-moment thing. This time she knew he wanted her, she wanted him, and they were going all the way to the finish line, consequences be damned.

Her hands climbed the outside length of his arms to clutch his shoulders. They were broad and strong and welcoming. She kneaded them for a moment before trailing her fingers around to the front of his shirt.

She didn't need to open her eyes or look at what she was doing to loosen the knot in his tie, unbutton his collar, then open the entire front of his starched white and pleated tuxedo shirt. He groaned as she touched his bare chest, and she was close to groaning with him.

The pads of her fingers dusted across hard and flat pectorals, tickled by just a sprinkling of crisp hair. Blast-furnace heat radiated from his skin and seeped into hers.

Pushing the sides of his shirt and jacket apart, she continued to explore, to study the contours of his body as though she were reading Braille. Then she ventured down to the waist of his pants.

Her nails raked his stomach and he sucked in a breath. Though her own breathing was none too steady and she was

gasping for air from their long, tortuous kiss, Lily grinned a
the feel of his abdomen going rigid at her touch. She traile
her fingers through the path of hair leading down the cente
and disappearing into his slacks.

With a groan, he took her mouth again, cupping the bac
of her head with both hands, stabbing his fingers through he
hair and against her scalp to anchor her in place.

She was only too happy to be there, to have him desperat
for her, out of control, ravishing her. She only wished they'
started earlier instead of wasting all that time on arguments
hurt feelings, uncertainty and explanations.

Finding his belt buckle, she worked it free, pulled the tw
ends apart and dragged the long strip of leather through it
loops in one fierce yank. It hit the floor with a thud a secon
before she went for the closure of his pants.

She could feel the heat of him, the hard, swollen lengt
pressing against the back of her hand through his fly. Sh
took a moment to run her knuckles up and down along th
prominent bulge, making Nigel moan and nip her lower li
with his teeth.

She smiled against his mouth, then let out a low moan o
her own when his hands slid down either side of her spine t
her bottom, squeezing roughly and tugging her even mor
firmly against his blatant arousal.

Squirming in his grip, she rubbed all along the front of hir
while at the same time wiggling her fingers between them t
undo the top of his pants and slowly ease down the zipper.

He let her work. Let her get as far as dipping her finger
tips beneath the waistband of his briefs before lifting his lip
from the pulse of her throat, setting her half a step away, an
tearing at the belt of her robe. It took him a moment to dea
with the knot, which got stuck from all his tugging. But the
it was loose, the edges of the robe falling open and catchin

at the bends of her arms when he pushed the plush material over her shoulders.

She was naked beneath, her flesh flushed pink now from passion rather than the steam of her shower. When the cool air of the suite hit her bare skin, she shivered. But she didn't try to pull her robe back up for warmth or try to cover her nudity. Not with Nigel standing there, staring at her as though she was the most delectable morsel ever created.

Not when she'd been dreaming about this moment for far too long. Wanted it far too much to hide.

So she stood there. Half-naked. Half shivering, both from the cool interior and the need coursing through her veins. And she let him look his fill.

Of course, while he was looking at her, she was returning the favor, taking in his surprisingly tanned skin against the backdrop of the white shirt and black tuxedo. His amazingly muscular and well-formed physique. He could have been a model posing for some sexy cologne ad—and raking in the dough when women everywhere flocked to buy whatever he was selling.

Though it felt like minutes, she was sure it only took a few seconds for them both to drink each other in, then lose all patience for the five or six inches that separated them. Nigel's hazel-green eyes glittered, reflecting the same desire she knew filled her own.

Lowering his head, his eyes grew hooded, and he made a feral sound deep in his throat before stalking toward her. He reached her in a blink, sweeping one arm around her back and the other behind her knees.

Her heart gave a little flutter as he lifted her against his chest in one smooth movement that didn't seem to tax him in the least. She released a breath of laughter and clutched his neck as he hiked her even higher.

He returned her grin, then leaned up to press his lips to

hers. Never breaking the kiss, he carried her across the room and straight to the waiting bed.

Once there, he balanced her carefully with one arm while reaching out to turn back the covers with his other hand. Then he laid her near the center of the soft mattress, following her down until he covered her like a warm, heavy human blanket.

The fabric of his tuxedo rubbed along her bare skin except where it was open down the front. The heat of his chest pressed to hers, making her want to wiggle and worm ever closer, if possible.

Wrapping her legs around him, she drove her hands inside his open shirt and tuxedo jacket, loosening it even further and pushing it jerkily over his shoulders and down his arms. He moved with her, aiding her efforts until he could shrug out of the garments and toss them aside.

Then he returned the favor, stroking her waist, her rib cage, the undersides of her breasts, but not lingering in any one spot, even though she writhed for his touch. Ignoring her whimpers of need, he finished removing her robe, lifting her when he needed to in order to tug the thick terry cloth out from under her. Then it, too, was gone, hitting the bureau with a *slap*.

His chest heaved as he stared down at her, his gaze raking from the top of her head to where her legs were still twined around his thighs. He took in her bare breasts, the slope of her belly, her triangle of feminine curls.

Everywhere he looked, she broke out in goose bumps. His nostrils flared, and his eyes flashed with a wolfish gleam.

Without taking his gaze from her, he kicked out of his pants and shoes and the rest of his clothes, dislodging her hold on him only when absolutely necessary. In seconds, he was naked and glorious, so beautiful he made her throat close with unexpected emotion. She swallowed it back as he moved over her. Reminded herself that this was just a casual fling, nothing more.

Lifting her arms, she wound them around his neck, drawing him to her even as he met her halfway. They kissed slowly, finally taking time to explore each other's mouths at a leisurely pace. The taste, the texture, likes and dislikes.

Of course, for her, it was all likes. And judging by the feel of him pressing against her inner thigh, he was liking everything just fine, as well.

His fingers tangled in her hair, angling her just the way he wanted while she raked his back, reveling in the play of muscle, the dip of his spine, the row of vertebrae leading down to the delectable swell of his ass.

His moan filled her mouth and his arms tightened around her. She arched into him, wanting to get close, even though they were already nearly as close as two people could be.

Dragging his lips across her cheek, he nipped at her throat, nibbled the lobe of her ear, trailed his mouth over her clavicle and toward her swollen, arched breasts.

Her breathing was choppy, her head getting fuzzier and fuzzier with longing as he teased her mercilessly and her temperature rose. But there were things that needed to be taken care of before they went much further. Before the fuzziness turned to full-blown mindlessness and she forgot everything but her own name.

"Nigel," she murmured, tightening her legs around his hips and moving her hands to his biceps while he nuzzled the side of her breast.

"Nigel," she said again when he didn't respond, resorting to tugging at his hair instead. "Condom. I don't have one— do you?"

It took a second for her words to sink in, for movements to slow and his mouth to halt mere centimeters from the center of her breast.

His head fell to the side and he groaned, the sound vibrating against her skin, making her shiver. With a particularly colorful-but-amusing curse of the British persuasion, he pushed himself up on his forearms to glare down at her.

Without waiting for her acquiescence, he peeled away from her and climbed out of the bed, flashing his sexy bare bottom as he hustled into the other room, where she assumed he had a stash of protection. Thank goodness, because she hadn't exactly packed for Los Angeles *or* Miami with hot, impulsive sex in mind.

Despite his command not to move a muscle, she pushed herself up on the bed, propping the pillows behind her and leaning against the bamboo headboard. She thought about tugging the sheet up to cover her stark nudity, then decided that if Nigel could stroll around the suite completely naked and unselfconscious, then she didn't have to be so modest, either.

He returned moments later, clutching a couple of distinctive plastic packets. Tossing one on the nightstand, he kept the other, tearing it open and quickly shaking out the contents.

Lily watched with barely suppressed eagerness as he sheathed himself in short, competent motions, then rejoined her on the bed, a dark, devilish gleam glinting in his eye as he closed in on her.

"I told you not to move."

His voice scraped like sandpaper, but still managed to pour over her in a rush of honeyed warmth.

She arched a brow, flashing him a wicked, unapologetic smile. "I guess I've been a bad girl. You may have to spank me."

Heat flared low in Nigel's belly, spreading outward until

it tingled in his limbs, pooled in his groin and flushed high across his cheekbones.

"Oh, I intend to do much more than that," he said in a voice gone arid with lust.

If he'd ever seen a more beautiful sight in his life than Lillian George sprawled naked in bed, waiting for him, he couldn't remember it. And now he didn't think he would ever forget.

As aroused as he was, as desperate as he was to be inside her, he couldn't seem to tear his gaze from the delightful picture she made. Her light brown hair falling loose around her shoulders, sexy and mussed from his fingers running through the long, silken strands. Her pale skin flushed with the rosy glow of desire.

Her breasts were small but perfect, their pale raspberry nipples puckered tight with arousal. And the rest of her was equally awe-inspiring—the slope of her waist, the triangle of blond curls at the apex of her thighs, the long, lean lines of her legs.

But what he loved most was her lack of inhibition. She didn't try to hide from him, didn't try to cover her nudity with her hands or a corner of the sheet. She was comfortable in her own skin. And more, she was comfortable with him, with what they were about to do with each other.

Feigning a patience and self-control he definitely didn't feel, he moved beside her, pulling her legs straight and tugging her into the cradle of his arms. She rolled against him, her breasts pressing flat to his chest, the arch of her foot rubbing lazily along his calf.

He brushed a loose curl away from her face, tucking it behind her ear. "In case I forget to mention it later, I'm awfully glad you agreed to come with me this weekend."

Her lips turned up at the corners, her blue eyes going soft and dewy. "Me, too."

"And though I don't mind sleeping in the other room, it will be nice to spend the night in this nice big bed, for a change."

She lifted one dainty brow at him. "I didn't say you could stay in bed with me."

He narrowed his eyes, fighting the twitch of his lips that threatened to pull them into a grin. "Planning to use me, then relegate me back to that dreadful cot, are you? Let's just see if I can change your mind about that."

He watched her mouth curve into a smile just before he kissed her. Her arms wrapped around his neck and trailed down his back as he shifted his weight, bringing her more snugly beneath him.

He'd meant what he'd said—bringing her along on this trip really had been one of his better ideas, even if he hadn't known at the time that they would end up here. He couldn't deny, however, that he'd hoped.

Almost from the first moment she'd walked into his office, every fiber of his being had shot to attention and begun imagining scenarios in which they ended up much like this. He'd known such a thing was dangerous, though, and couldn't—or shouldn't—happen.

But now that it was…he couldn't bring himself to be sorry. Or to worry about the consequences. All he wanted was to continue kissing her, caressing her, making love to her all night long.

And if she thought to send him back to that cramped, lumpy roll-away bed after she'd gained her satisfaction… Well, he would just have to keep her so busy and blinded by passion that she lost all track of the time. He would be spending the night in her bed before she even realized the sun was coming up.

He stroked the smooth roundness of her shoulders, her

arms, her back. Everywhere he could reach while their tongues continued to mate. He could kiss her forever and never grow bored. But there was so much more he wanted to do with her.

With a small groan of reluctance, he lightened the kiss, drawing away just enough to nibble at the corner of her mouth, trailing down her chin to her throat. She threw her head back, giving him even better access. He took his time licking his way down, pressing his lips to her pulse, dipping his tongue into the hollow at the very center, where he felt her swallow.

They rolled slightly so that he was lying over her again, and she welcomed him by hitching her legs high on his hips and locking her ankles at the small of his spine. It brought him flush with her feminine warmth, and brought a groan of longing snaking up from the depths of his diaphragm.

Her fingers kneaded his biceps while he turned his attention to her lovely, lovely breasts. The nipples called to him: tight little cherries atop perfectly shaped mounds of pillowy-soft flesh. He squeezed and stroked with his hands while his lips circled first one pert tip and then the other.

Beneath him, Lillian wiggled impatiently and made tiny mewling sounds while his mouth grew bolder. He kissed and licked and suckled, trying to give each breast equal consideration until the press of her moist heat against his nearly painful arousal grew too distracting to ignore.

Lifting his head, he pressed a quick, hard kiss to her mouth. "There's so much I want to do to you," he murmured, brushing her lips, her cheekbone, the curve of her brow with the pad of his thumb. "So much time I want to spend just touching you, learning every inch of your body. But we may have to wait until later for all of the slow, leisurely stuff. Right now I simply need you too much."

He canted his hips, nudging her with the tip of his erection to emphasize his point. Bowing into him, she brought them into even fuller, more excruciating contact. He hissed out a breath, closing his eyes and praying for the endurance to make it through this night and shag her properly without embarrassing himself.

To his shocked delight, she clutched his buttocks with both hands and leaned up to nip his chin with her teeth. "I'm all for fast first. Slow is overrated."

Nigel chuckled, wondering how he'd gotten so bloody lucky. Hugging her to him, he kissed her again, melding their mouths the way he fully intended to meld their bodies.

Skating a palm down the outside of her thigh, he hitched her leg higher on his hip, opening her to him and settling his sheathed arousal directly against her cleft. He sucked in a breath as her moist heat engulfed him as though the thin layer of latex wasn't even there.

If he was this affected, this close to the edge just by resting against her so intimately, what would happen once he began to penetrate her? Once he was seated to the hilt, with her tight, feminine walls constricted around him? He was almost afraid to find out, and imagined something along the lines of the top of his head flying off and consciousness deserting him entirely.

Lillian ran her fingers into his hair, raking his scalp and tugging his mouth down to hers. Impatiently, she writhed against him, inviting him in, making it more than clear what she wanted.

Peppering him with a series of biting kisses, she murmured, "Stop teasing, Nigel. Do it already."

He would have chuckled at her less-than-eloquent demand if he wasn't just as desperate for her. Sliding a hand between their bodies, he did tease her, enough to draw a ragged moan from deep in her throat. But only to test her readiness and be sure she could accommodate him.

Gritting his teeth, he found her center and pressed forward. She was tight and hot, but took him willingly, inch by tantalizing inch. Their panting breaths and staccato moans echoed through the room while he sank as far as he could go. Filling her, torturing himself.

She fit him like a glove—silken, warm, heavenly. It was a bliss he could have easily spent the rest of the night savoring. If only he hadn't been so desperate to move, the fire, the desire racing through his veins. Lillian's teeth at his earlobe, her softly whispered encouragement, and the way she spoke his name on such a breathy sigh let him know she felt the same.

His whole body taut with need, he drew back. Sliding forward. Slow, even motions that brought exquisite pleasure even as the impulse to thrust faster and harder grew.

Mewling in his ear, Lillian's arms tightened around his neck, her legs around his waist. Her breasts rubbed eagerly against his chest, spurring him on.

"Nigel," she murmured into his neck. The sound of his name on her lips, the feel of them on his skin sent pleasure skating down his spine.

"Please," she begged, slanting her hips, driving him deeper. It was a request, or possibly even a demand, for more.

With a growl he gripped her hips and began to move in earnest. Long, slow strokes followed by short, fast ones. Then the opposite—long and fast, short and slow.

He mixed it up, throwing off any semblance of gentlemanly behavior in an effort to increase pleasure and bring them both to a rocketing completion. With luck, he would be able to hold back his own orgasm long enough to see that Lillian was well-pleased first, though that was becoming more and more of a priority.

And then she started bucking beneath him, her nails raking his back as she cried out. His name, a plea, a litany of *yes, yes, yes, yes.*

Fever heated his blood to a boil while he silently joined in her chorus of need. His muscles tensed, grew rigid. Slipping a hand between them, he drifted his fingers through her downy curls and found the tiny bud of pleasure hidden there.

At the very first touch, Lillian threw her head back and screamed, convulsing around him. Nigel plunged deep, again and again, wanting to prolong the ecstasy, but having no control over millions of volts of electricity setting off fireworks beneath his skin and low, low in his gut.

With a heartfelt groan, he stiffened inside of her, thrusting one last time as ecstasy exploded behind his eyes and spread outward to every cell and nerve ending.

Long, silent moments passed while his heart pounded beneath his rib cage and they both tried to school their breathing. Sweat dotted their skin, sealing them together as he rolled them carefully to one side.

He kept an arm around her, one of her legs thrown over his hip. Her riot of wavy brown hair spilled across the pillow beneath her head, and he smiled, reaching out to pluck a stray strand from where it was stuck to her lips.

At the featherlight touch, she blinked dreamily and opened cornflower-blue eyes to stare up at him.

"Mmm," rolled from her lips in a throaty purr.

Nigel chuckled. "I'll take that as a sign that I left you moderately speechless."

Her mouth curved in contented acquiescence, her eyes fluttering closed again.

Assuming she'd drifted off to sleep, he extricated himself from their tangle of arms and legs and padded to the loo to dispose of the condom and clean up. Returning to the bed, he crawled in beside her, arranged the covers over their still-naked bodies and pulled her back into his arms once again.

She snuggled against him, resting her head on his shoulder and throwing one of her legs over his thigh. Amazingly, the close proximity had arousal stirring to life a second time. But more than mere desire, a warm wash of satisfaction seeped through him unlike anything he'd ever felt before after what was supposed to be only a casual, rushed sexual encounter.

He'd known Lillian George was different—special even— from the first time he'd seen her. He just hadn't known how special, and he wasn't certain even now. All he knew was that she evoked emotions in him he couldn't remember ever feeling before. And created thoughts in his head that he'd never before been tempted to consider.

Stirring beside him, Lillian turned her face up to his, letting her eyes fall open a crack. Her breath danced across his skin and she made a low humming sound deep in her throat before parting her lips to speak.

"I changed my mind," she said drowsily. "You can sleep in the bed with me, after all."

Considering that he was already quite near to doing that already, he couldn't help but chuckle.

"Why thank you," he said, doing his best to feign gratitude when what he really felt was amusement. "That's terribly generous of you."

"I'm a generous person," she mumbled, but he could tell she really was slipping off to sleep this time.

He pressed a kiss to her forehead, waiting until her breathing became fluid and even. "I hope so," he murmured more to himself than to her. "I certainly hope so."

Eleven

They woke up just in the nick of time the next morning. Nigel counted himself lucky they'd woken up at all, considering how…active they'd been throughout the night.

They'd made love once, twice…he'd lost track at three. And that didn't include the time he'd stirred her from sleep by lapping at her honeyed sweetness and pleasuring her with his mouth. Or the time she'd awakened him by returning the favor.

Which made it a miracle that they were up now, dressed quite fashionably, and on their way to the charity runway show that was scheduled to start in a little under two hours, without looking like the walking dead. He was wearing a simple tan suit, white dress shirt open at the throat in deference to both Miami's weather and its casual, oceanside style of dress. It had taken him all of twenty minutes to shower and get ready.

It had taken Lillian slightly longer, but the added time had been well worth it given the results. Her hair was a mass of pale brown waves, drawn up at the sides and held in place while the rest fell down her back in a loose, sexy ponytail. Her makeup was light and flawless, showing no underlying signs of her lack of rest. And she was wearing a short, brightly flowered sundress that definitely hadn't come from the Ashdown Abbey collection. It was, however, perfect for the Florida sunshine, and she looked good enough to eat.

He rather wished he could skip the fashion show altogether, drag her back to the hotel suite and do just that. It took a number of stern mental lectures and dressings-down to keep from telling their driver to turn around and return them to the Royal Crown.

He was Ashdown Abbey's CEO, after all; he was required to be there. And as upset as his father was already with the company's performance since opening stores and a manufacturing plant in the United States, he doubted the old man would be happy to hear Nigel had blown off a big event to spend the day setting the sheets afire with his lovely new personal assistant.

But despite all the reasons he knew he couldn't, he still wanted to. Especially when he reached for her hand in the lift on the way down to the car and she let him take it, leaving her fingers in his on the walk through the lobby, then again in the limousine. And when she sat mere inches from him in the back of the car—still a respectable distance, but much closer than she had the previous night.

They arrived at the event location and joined a line of vehicles waiting to discharge their passengers. People were pouring into the giant white tent set up for the runway show. Slowly, the limo moved forward until it was at the head of the line, and the driver came around to open the door and let them out.

Nigel stepped out first, then assisted Lillian, keeping her

close to his side while camera lenses approached and flashes of light went off all around them. Today's show wasn't exactly a red-carpet event, but there were enough big-name designers showing and celebrities in attendance that it brought out a crowd of paparazzi and legitimate media alike.

Nigel smiled, nodded, played the part, all the while guiding Lillian through the throng with nothing more than a hand at her back. He was careful not to touch her anywhere else or give any hint to the public of the true nature of their relationship. Or what could be considered the true nature of their relationship after the way they'd spent last evening, at any rate.

It seemed to take forever to make it through the tent, stopping every few feet to say hello or speak to people he knew, people who wanted to know him, or simply big associates it was best to share pleasantries with. Until finally they reached their reserved seating near the runway.

Before sitting down, Nigel took Lillian's hand and leaned close to whisper in her ear. "I need to go backstage and check on preparations for the show. Would you like to come with me or stay here?"

Her fingers tightened around his and she looked more excited than he would have expected, her eyes lighting with anticipation. "I'll go, if that's all right," she replied.

He led her along the long, long frame of the raised runway, weaving around bystanders and finding the entrance to the rear staging area tucked off to one side. Backstage was a mad mass of wall-to-wall people rushing here and there, yelling, calling out, trying to hear and be heard over the cacophony of noise and other voices.

He had a general idea of where the Ashdown Abbey staff and collection were set up, and headed that way.

When they reached the proper area, models were at different stages of hair and makeup and dressing in the chosen Ashdown Abbey designs that would be walking the runway today.

At the center of it all stood the head designer of the collection, Michael Franklin. Calling out instructions, pointing this way and that, keeping everyone on task. As frantic as it looked, Nigel knew from past runway shows that it was all a sort of controlled chaos. Once everything was ready and the show was underway, Michael and everyone else would sit back and declare that things had gone off with nary a hitch.

When the designer spotted Nigel and Lillian standing at the edge of the activity, he lowered his arms, took a deep breath and bustled over. *Time to put on a confident air for the boss,* Nigel thought with amusement. Though he wasn't the least alarmed by what he was witnessing. In his experience, what was taking place behind the scenes of the runway was perfectly normal, Michael Franklin perfectly capable of choreographing the necessary stages of preparation.

"Mr. Statham," Franklin greeted, shaking Nigel's hand.

Nigel said hello and reintroduced him to Lillian before asking how everything was going.

"Fine, fine," Franklin replied. "We're short one model, though," he added, glancing to see if she might be somewhere in the crush of people surrounding them. "I'm sure she'll be here, but if she doesn't show up soon, we'll be pushing back the prep for the champagne gown. We had special hair and accessories lined up for it, since it's our final design to walk the runway."

Nigel pursed his lips, wondering if he should put voice to the idea flashing through his head. It was brilliant, of course, at least to his mind. But he wasn't so certain Franklin or Lillian would agree.

Mistaking his drawn brows for upset, Franklin rushed to reassure him. "Don't worry, Mr. Statham, everything is under control. We'll get the model here or find another. If I have to, *I'll* squeeze into the dress and walk it out there myself."

"Actually," Nigel said, deciding to take a chance Lillian

wouldn't slap him for his presumptuousness with so many witnesses standing around, "I have a thought about that myself." Turning to Lillian, he took her arm encouragingly "Why don't you stand in for the missing model?"

Her eyes went wide, her face pale.

"What? No. Don't be ridiculous."

"What's so ridiculous about it?" he argued. "You're beautiful, poised, more than capable. And we both know you look amazing in the gown, since you wore it to the cocktail party just last night. I'd say it's an ideal solution."

Before she had the chance to say anything more, he turned back to Franklin. "Send her to hair and makeup and get her into the dress. Make sure she looks like a million bucks. She'll be the perfect close to our portion of the show."

"Nigel," Lillian said, shaking her head, looking on the verge of panic.

He leaned in, pressing a kiss to her cheek. "You'll be fine, he assured her. "Better than fine, you'll be marvelous."

When she still didn't look convinced, he added, "Please We need your help."

He heard her sigh, knew she was on the verge of acquiescence and didn't give her a chance to change her mind.

"Go," he commanded, pushing her toward Franklin pleased when the man wasted no time grabbing her up and bustling her off to get ready.

With a smile on his face and heady anticipation thrumming through his veins, he made his way back out front, taking his seat and awaiting what he suspected would be the best runway show of his life. Career aspects be damned.

Hours later, Lily was still shaking. She'd never been so nervous in her life. Not even on her first day pretending to be a personal assistant for Nigel.

What had he been thinking? She wasn't a model. Far from

t. She was a designer, for heaven's sake. Her place was well on the other side of fashion—behind the scenes, not out in front, walking a runway with hundreds of eyes riveted on her and flashbulbs going off in her face every tenth of a second.

Not that Nigel was aware of any of that. But that still didn't give him the right to dress her up and shove her out there without warning.

She'd survived, of course. She even liked to think she'd done an exceptional job. At least she'd stayed on her feet, hadn't fainted and had made it all the way down the runway and back without falling off into the crowd of onlookers.

But what if someone recognized her? From the audience or later, from all of the pictures and video clips that were sure to be circulating across the globe.

Too many people knew her as Lily Zaccaro. Even with her hair a little darker than her natural shade and heavier makeup than usual for the runway, somebody out there was sure to notice her and wonder what she'd been doing walking the runway for one of her competitors.

With luck, they would call her cell phone to ask what was going on. But much more likely, they would call the apartment and end up talking to either Juliet or Zoe. Her sisters would be clueless, but they'd begin to put two and two together, track her down in Los Angeles and blow her entire use as Lillian George.

Nigel would be furious—for good reason. But worse, she would be kicked out of Ashdown Abbey. Before she'd figured out who was stealing her designs.

Dammit. How did she get herself into these predicaments?

Running her fingers through her hair, she shook it out of its overly sprayed upsweep until it resembled at least a modicum of normal, natural, non-runway style. She was out of the champagne-colored gown and back in the sundress she'd been wearing when they first arrived.

The makeup, however, would have to remain until they re
turned to the hotel suite and she could take some cotton ball
and about ten gallons of makeup remover to it. Not that sh
looked like a clown. It was just that everything—eyeline
shadow, mascara, blush, lipstick—was thicker and heavie
than usual to be seen from a distance and on camera.

She was about to turn away from the oversize mirror an
head back out front when a pair of hands spanned her wais
and warm lips pressed against the side of her neck. Her gaz
flicked to her reflection, and now Nigel's, close behind her

"You were wonderful," he spoke near her ear, barely abov
a whisper. "I knew you would be."

Stepping away before someone noticed his familiarity wit
the person who was supposed to be simply his personal as
sistant, he added, "That model never did show up, so than
you for saving the show."

"You're welcome," she said with a touch of reluctance
Then she turned to face him, crossing her arms and hitchin
one hip in annoyance. "You might have *asked* if I wanted t
play supermodel before pushing me out onstage against m
will. Do you have any idea how petrified I was? You're luck
I didn't throw up on one of the other models or pass out righ
in the middle of the runway and ruin the whole show."

To her surprise, he chuckled at her aggravation, a wid
smile stretching across his handsome features.

"Nonsense. You were exceptional. And I can't imagin
anyone else looking as lovely in that gown…not even a pro
fessional model paid to look good in designer creations."

As much as she wanted to hold on to her mad, his flat
tery was working. She was glad she'd been able to help out i
such a way when he'd needed her, happy that he was please
with her performance.

But that didn't change the fact that she was in trouble. Ba

enough they'd slept together last night. That she wanted it to—*hoped* it would, even—happen again.

Now she needed to worry about someone recognizing her and figuring out what she was doing playing out a second identity. That *Nigel* might realize what she was up to and hate her forever.

Her heart gave a painful lurch. She might be lying to him. What they had might be casual, temporary and doomed to be short-lived. But the thought of him finding out who she really was, what she'd been doing pretending to be his personal assistant all this time, nearly brought tears to her eyes.

An ill-fated romantic fling she could handle. Seeing a look of betrayal, possibly even disgust, in his eyes after what they'd shared... No, she didn't want her time with him to end like that.

Which meant she needed to be very careful from this point on. She needed to guard herself against any further attachment to this man. Whatever else transpired between them, she couldn't let it affect her emotionally.

Most importantly, though, she needed to get back to the Ashdown Abbey offices in Los Angeles and find out once and for all who stole her designs for the California Collection.

Oblivious to the twisting, hazard-strewn path her thoughts were taking, he ran his hands down her bare arms, threading his fingers with hers. "If you're ready, we can go. We'll have to make pleasantries as we weave our way through the crowd out there, but the car is waiting to take us back to the hotel."

"Don't you need to stick around awhile?" she asked. "Rub elbows and talk up the company to key account holders?"

"Already done," he replied. "I spoke to several buyers just after the show, while you were changing back into street clothes, and anyone else who might be interested in acquiring our designs has my card. They can call me at the office on Monday."

"That was quick," she said. "I would have thought you'd need to spend the rest of the day schmoozing."

He offered her a gentle smile. "Sometimes I do. But for the most part, these types of events drag on for the public's enjoyment. Those of us who are there for business tend to know each other, look for each other and get straight to the point. Besides," he said, leaning in and lowering his voice to a sultry whisper, "I don't want to be stuck out there, making nice with mere strangers, when I could spend the rest of my time in Miami alone with you."

A flush of longing washed over her, making her catch her breath. She licked her lips, waiting until she thought she could speak without sounding like Kermit the Frog.

"So," she said carefully, "we'll be headed back to Los Angeles soon?"

"Tomorrow. But that gives us the rest of the day and this evening to enjoy the sand and sun."

She cocked her head, unable to keep her mouth from quirking up at one side. "The sand and sun, or our suite back at the Royal Crown?"

He returned her grin with a wink and wicked twinkle to his hazel-green eyes. "I'll let that be your choice, of course. Though I know which I'm hoping for."

She shook her head and chuckled, unable to resist his inherent charm. The man was entirely too tempting for his own good. Or hers.

And though it might not have been the wisest decision for her to make, especially given her current situation, she *wanted* to spend the night with him. Another night, just the two of them alone together.

While she realized it would essentially be digging herself even deeper into her deception and making it that much harder to walk away, she wanted as much time alone with him as she

ould get. Secret minutes, private hours, cherished memories
o carry with her the rest of her life.

She might not have a future with Nigel—how could she
when she'd been lying to him ever since they met?—but
he could have this. The here and now. And if that was all she
ould lay claim to, then she was going to grab on with both
ands and savor it for all it was worth.

"All right," she told him slowly, teasing him a little. "I'll
ell you what. You can take me to lunch, and I'll let you know
fterward what I want to do next."

He gave her a look, one that said he intended to do every-
hing in his power to convince her to make the right deci-
ion. The one that led straight back to their hotel suite and
nded with them both sweaty, naked, wrapped together like
udzu vines.

She shivered a little at the slideshow of pictures that
an through her head. Oh, yes, they would get there. But it
vouldn't hurt to make him worry a bit about the day's out-
ome first.

Turning in the opposite direction toward the curtained-
ff entrance between backstage and the show area, he of-
ered his arm. As she took it and they started walking, he
aid, "Fair enough. Just remember that I haven't quite got-
en my fair share of time in that big bed back at the hotel.
t would be a shame to fly home before I've gotten to use
: properly."

Lily bit down on the inside of her cheek to keep from
aughing aloud. The campaign to spend the rest of their time
n Miami safely ensconced in the suite had begun already,
: seemed. Although she didn't see why they had to restrict
heir activities to the bed he was so preoccupied with. After
ll, there was also the sofa, the desk, the balcony, the shower,
he bathroom vanity...

Leaning into him, despite the fact that someone might see

and perceive that there was more going on between them tha mere boss-and-secretary professional relations, she said, "I' keep that in mind."

The sofa, the desk, the bathroom vanity, the shower an the bed. They'd hit every place but the balcony, at least i part, before checking out of the hotel Sunday morning an boarding the jet back to Los Angeles.

Lily knew how dangerous it was to let herself get so car ried away with Nigel. Had reprimanded herself several time while locked away with him, doing all the things she told her self she shouldn't. But she just didn't have it in her to sto before she absolutely had to, so she'd decided to adopt a don' ask-don't-tell attitude. She wouldn't ask herself why she wa letting things go on this way when she knew how they wer going to end, and she wouldn't tell herself later what a foo she'd been for letting her time at Ashdown Abbey and he feelings for Nigel Statham get out of control.

Which was how she ended up agreeing to have room ser vice deliver lunch after the runway show instead of eating i a lovely, public five-star restaurant so they could spend mor time together, alone in the suite. And how she allowed him t sit so close to her on the flight home, interspersing busines talk with naughty whispers about his favorite parts of wha they'd done together and what he'd very much like to do in th future. Not the far distant future, but soon after they landec

As hard as she tried to resist, she even let him talk her int going home with him from the airport. It was a terrible idea One that could only get her deeper into the hole she was dig ging for herself. The same hole that was quickly filling wit quicksand, threatening to pull her under.

But there was something about his fingers trailing alon her bare thigh just beneath the hem of her skirt...his warr breath dusting her ear, sending ripples of sensation all th way down to her toes. It stirred up too many memories from their time locked away together in the hotel suite, and made her weak and susceptible and eager to make more.

So she let herself be persuaded. Let him lead her from the jet to his waiting Bentley, let him *not* drop her off at her apartment, but take her home with him instead, her heart in her throat the entire drive.

She'd expected some dazzling but garish mansion in Beverly Hills, complete with swimming pool and a home bowling alley or some such. Instead, he led her past a uniformed doorman into a very nice redbrick apartment building not far from the Ashdown Abbey offices. Definitely a few steps up from the one where she was staying, especially when she discovered—of course—that his was the penthouse apartment.

The view was spectacular, as were the layout and furnishings. Not his own, he'd explained; he'd rented it that way, but they suited him perfectly nonetheless. A lot of chrome and glass and neutral colors, interspersed with splashes of bright color.

He gave her all of ten minutes to process her surroundings while his chauffer brought in their luggage and he poured them each a glass of wine. Then he'd led her to the bedroom, where he'd proceeded to give her the grand tour of his king-size bed, ocean-blue satin sheets and the eggshell paint of the ceiling over her head.

He'd kept her there for hours…not that she'd minded. Then when she began making noises about going home to her own apartment, he'd insisted she stay for dinner. She'd refused, at least until he'd offered to cook. That was something she just *had* to see.

Unfortunately, she'd also had to eat it with a smile on her face, since she hadn't had the heart to tell him his culinary skills needed work.

After that, he'd very deftly seduced her again, keepin
her distracted and too exhausted to protest until mornin
Of course, in the morning, they'd had to go into the office.

Thankfully, she'd had enough clothes with her from th
trip that she hadn't had to wear the same thing two days in
row. And Nigel had been kind enough to drop her off a cou
ple of blocks from the Ashdown Abbey building so it looke
as though she'd arrived by herself, then followed behind se
eral minutes later.

From there, they'd proceeded to fool around in his offic
exchange heated glances even when they weren't alone, and-
to Lily's consternation and self-reproach—practically mov
in together. It was comfortable and a lot easier a routine t
fall into than she would have expected. At the very least, sh
found herself spending entirely too much time in Nigel's pre
ence and sleeping over at his penthouse.

Time she was spending getting swept up in the fantasy c
spending the rest of her life with this man, inching ever clos
to the edge of falling for him once and for all. But *not* ge
ting any closer to discovering the thief of her designs. Ever
minute she was with Nigel was one she didn't use to snoc
around or pore through Ashdown Abbey records.

After nearly a week of sneaking around at work, of the
acting like boss and secretary with a professional relation
ship only, then using the evening hours to act like a couple c
randy teenagers—or worse, star-crossed lovers in some rc
mantic chick flick—Lily realized she had to get back on trac

She considered herself extremely lucky that nothing ha
ever seemed to come of her jaunt down the runway in Miam
Apparently, everyone—even the media—had been more fc
cused on the debut designs than who was wearing them. An
the big hair and heavy makeup had certainly helped.

Because no one had ever called to ask what she'd bee
doing there, or pointed at a photograph from the show ar

mmented that one of the Ashdown Abbey models looked
awful lot like that Zaccaro chick from New York.

Thank goodness.

But even if she couldn't bring herself to break things off
ith Nigel entirely, she did manage to clear her head enough
insist on spending the night at her own apartment for a
ange. *Without* him joining her there.

Lily hadn't taken her personal cell phone with her to Flor-
a, only the one provided to her by Ashdown Abbey for com-
ny business. And she'd been so distracted by her impromptu
ay at Nigel's penthouse that she'd forgotten to grab it the
ngle time she'd managed to swing by her own apartment.
was still in the nightstand beside her neatly made, narrow
vin bed, exactly where she'd left it.

So when she finally got inside her apartment, alone, and
as able to take a breath, clear her head and focus again,
e found her voice-mail box full. As soon as she turned the
one on, it started beeping with notification after notifica-
n that she had messages waiting.

Suspecting what she would hear and who most of them
ould be from, she almost didn't want to listen, but knew
e had to. Kicking off her heels, she moved around the liv-
g room, gathering papers and folders and notebooks even
she dialed in for the messages.

Sure enough, several were from her sister Juliet. *Where*
e you? Why didn't you say where you were going in your
te? Why haven't you called me back? Please call me back.
e're worried about you. Where are you?

Lily's heart hurt more with each message, guilt biting at
r as her sister's voice grew more and more frantic.

Then there were the ones from her private investigator,
eid McCormack. He was anything but frantic. In fact, he
unded downright furious, and darned if Lily could figure
t why. He worked for her, after all. Shouldn't *she* be the

one to get upset at his lack of progress rather than the oth
way around?

But while his first couple of voice mails were poli
enough, simply requesting an update or letting her know he
found no connection between Ashdown Abbey and the the
of her designs in New York, they quickly deteriorated in
demands for her to return his calls and threats to put an end
their association if she didn't soon come clean with her sister

She rubbed the spot between her brows, massaging awa
the beginning of a headache. This was all supposed to be
simple, and now it was so complicated. She was supposed
be the only one involved, at risk, and now things had sprea
to encompass so many others. People she cared about an
wanted to protect.

With a sigh, she glanced at the phone's display and did th
math for the difference between West Coast and East Coa
time. If she waited just a little longer, she might be able
call the apartment back in New York and leave a message f
her sisters when neither of them would be home. That wou
give her the chance to reassure them—especially Juliet—th
she was fine and hoped to be home soon without having
explain where she was or what she was really up to.

Because if Juliet or Zoe answered, there would be no er
to the number of questions they would ask. They'd grill h
like a toasted-cheese sandwich, and she just *couldn't* tell the
the whole truth. Not yet.

Which brought her to the next and most important item o
her must-do list. She *had* to figure out how Ashdown Abb
had gotten enough of a peek at her designs to incorpora
them into their California Collection.

Tossing all of the paperwork she'd gathered so far fro
the annals of Ashdown Abbey on the coffee table in front
the sofa, she trailed into the bedroom and changed from th
sundress and sandals she'd worn home from Florida to a pa

f comfortable cotton pajamas. Then she returned to the front
oom, started a pot of coffee—which she suspected would
e only the first of many—and hunkered down on the floor
cross-legged, with her back to the couch.

Given all the snooping she'd already done and information
he'd collected, Lily didn't understand why she couldn't figure out who the design thief was. It had to be there, buried,
idden, eluding her. Worse, she felt as though the answer was
right there, just out of reach. If only she knew exactly where
o look…or exactly what she was looking for.

What she needed was a second set of eyes. Her sisters—
uliet, at any rate—would be terrific at poring through the
ages and pages of data. But hadn't the entire point been *not*
o get her sisters involved?

The detective would be another excellent choice. But Ju-
iet had contacted him right after Lily had, and now he was
mack in the middle of a conflict of interest. From his per-
pective, anyway—not from Lily's, and she hoped not from
uliet's once she found out what was really going on. It did
xplain Reid McCormack's souring disposition, though.

On the heels of that thought came another wave of guilt.
All right, all right, she told her nagging conscience. Grabbing
er cell phone, she dialed McCormack's office number first.
The better to *not* catch him and be able to leave a message
e could listen to later…when she wasn't on the other end of
he line, a cornered recipient of his wrath.

And thankfully, it was his voice mail rather than his real
ive voice that answered.

"Mr. McCormack, this is Lily Zaccaro," she said. Quickly,
uccinctly, knowing she didn't have much time before the
ystem cut her off and wanting to sound very sure of her-
elf, she continued, "I'm sorry I haven't contacted you, but
got your messages and promise I'm nearly done here. I'm
ot going to give her any details about my whereabouts, but

I will call Juliet and let her know I'm okay. And I'll explai
everything as soon as I get back to New York. I'm sorry
this is causing you problems, but please don't say anythin
to my sisters—not yet. Thank you."

Heart racing, she hung up, hoping she'd said the righ
things. Hoping she'd bought herself a little more time an
extinguished at least a bit of his anger with her.

She thought about calling her sister next, but it was Sunda
afternoon, and though the store was open, the three of ther
usually took that day off. The chances of both Juliet and Zo
being home were too high. She would wait until tomorrov
when the two of them *should* be back at the boutique and ur
able to answer the apartment phone. Her message would b
waiting for them when they got home, though, which shoul
make them feel better about her health and welfare.

That decided, she went back to flipping through paper
and her notes, studying each carefully, just as she had sev
eral times before. The letters were starting to blur togethe
the words branding themselves in her brain. And yet she wa
clearly missing something or the mystery would have bee
solved by now.

For the next few hours, she kept at it, sipping coffee to sta
alert as she organized and reorganized, straightened and re
straightened. Sighed and sighed again.

She was going over the specifics of the California Collection—
memos, instructions, supply lists and sketches—when somethin
caught her attention. Sitting up straight, she leaned forward eve
as she brought the printout in her hand closer.

Down in the far left corner, in teeny-tiny print smaller tha
a footnote, was a number. Or rather, a resource code, wit
numbers and letters mixed together: CA_COLL-47N6BL92

It meant absolutely nothing to her, except that it seeme
to be an identifier for the California Collection. And like on
of those 3-D magic mystery image puzzles, she might neve

ave seen it if exhaustion wasn't making her eyes cross and
ision blur.

Grabbing up the next page, she glanced down and found
he exact same thing. And on the next. And on the next. And
n the next.

Her pulse jumped in anticipation. This could actually
e something. Of course, she didn't know exactly what and
vasn't even sure how to find out.

But on a hunch, she ran for her laptop, popped the lid and
ooted up. Thanks to her position as executive secretary/
ersonal assistant to the Man in Charge at Ashdown Abbey,
he had all the log-in information to tap into the computer
ystem from home—which she'd done numerous times after
ours as part of her amateur investigation.

Once she was in, it took her twenty, maybe twenty-five
ninutes just to locate anything even remotely related to the
ode, and another ten or fifteen to track down what the jum-
le of letters and numbers meant.

It was, she discovered, an identifier for all of the sketches
nd other information related to the California Collection.
And miraculously, it brought her to a compilation of scans of
he original sketches for the California Collection.

They were definitely rougher sketches than the ones she'd
een studying all this time, done by hand in charcoal and
olored pencil and with computerized drawing pads and the
ike. All grouped together, they were miniscule, but thank-
ully she was able to enlarge them and even run them across
er screen in a slideshow fashion.

A flare of annoyance raised Lily's temperature several de-
rees. If she'd thought the final results of the collection were
imilar to her work, the original sketches were practically car-
on copies. Someone had initially pitched almost her *exact*
reations, and they had somehow—thank heavens for small

favors, she now realized—been transformed into garment
more suitable to Ashdown Abbey.

Refocusing her attention away from her fit of temper, sh
began to scan every detail of the designs and right away no
ticed that each of them was signed with the same set of ini
tials.

IOL.

Lily's brows knit. So often with design teams, no one too
or was given full credit for initial ideas. She'd suspecte
someone of using her designs as suggestions for aspects o
the California Collection, but not that a single person had of
fered up complete, nearly identical sketches for all of the de
signs, which had then been applied to the overall collection

Apparently, she'd been going at her little investigation al
wrong from the very beginning. The thought made her wan
to smack her head on the nearest hard surface, even as sh
admitted a newfound respect for folks like Reid McCormack
who did this sort of thing professionally. Clearly, she wa
better off locked in her studio with bolts of fabric and threa
in every color than out in the world playing amateur sleuth

Not that she could quit now. She'd come too far and wa
finally, *finally* on the verge of figuring out this whole ugl
mess.

It took a minute or two more of tapping at the keyboard
but she found the entire list of employees connected to th
California Collection and started scrolling through. No one
no one with the initials IOL that she could see. Dammit.

Teeth grinding in frustration, she drummed her fingers o
the coffee table and tried to think of what to do next.

Bingo! Payroll records.

Accessing the human resources files, she found the re
cord of every single employee working at Ashdown Abbey
regardless of his or her position. From Nigel as CEO all th
way down to the custodial team that came in nightly to clea

e offices, she scrolled through every single name, looking
r one to match to those three initials.

A ton of *L* surnames popped up, only a few first names
at started with the letter *I*. But she kept going, holding her
reath in hopes that the mysterious IOL would pop up and
te her on the nose.

And there it was. Her fingers paused on the touch pad,
opping the document's movement. She blew out a breath
ven as her stomach plummeted and her heart hammered
ainst her rib cage.

Isabelle Olivia Landry. IOL.

Bella.

Lily leaned back against the edge of the sofa, feeling all
e blood drain from her face. Bella? Zoe's friend Bella?

Sure, the thought had crossed her mind—*briefly*—after
ey'd run into one another, but she'd never truly believed
ything like that could be possible.

Could she really have done this? To her friend…her friend's
sters…her friend's company?

Why would she have done such a thing? And how did she
anage it?

It made sense, though, didn't it? The longer Lily thought
out it, went back in her memory, the more things began to
ll into place.

Bella and Zoe were friends. Bella had visited Zoe not all
at long ago. She'd stayed at the loft with them, toured the
onnected studio where they worked from home and the space
here they worked in the back of the store, too, she was sure.

She couldn't blame Zoe for showing her friend around,
ther. Lily and Juliet had both given tours to friends, shar-
 g their work space as well as designs they were currently
orking on. None of them would ever think a *friend* would
eal their ideas and try to pass them off as their own or sell
em to another designer.

No, this betrayal lay solely at Bella's feet. But Lily still wanted to know how she'd managed it. And *why*.

Had she memorized so much from just a casual glance, or had she sneaked around behind their backs and literally stole designs, perhaps traced or copied them to take away with her

Tears pricked behind Lily's eyes even as her finger clenched. She was sad and angry at the same time. Relieved to have the mystery solved, but dreading what was to com

Because she had to confront Bella now, didn't she?

Or maybe she shouldn't. Maybe she should turn over all this evidence to the police. Or Reid McCormack so he could investigate further and gather even more evidence again Bella.

Gather even more evidence. So that they—she—could prosecute someone who at one time had been a close frien of her sister's. The very thought made her want to throw u

But it had to be done, didn't it? Even though now that she knew the truth, it felt like rather a hollow victory.

And yet it was the whole reason she'd run away from hom in the first place. Left without telling her family where she was going and sent poor Juliet into such turmoil over he whereabouts…flown to Los Angeles and gotten a job with rival clothing company under an assumed name…let herse get carried away by her feelings for Nigel and fall into an a fair with him that was going to end badly…so badly.

If she didn't take action against Bella for stealing her d signs, all that would be for naught.

Wouldn't it?

Twelve

There were some things makeup couldn't hide, and the shadows under Lily's eyes were two of them. She couldn't remember ever spending a worse, more sleepless night in her life.

For hours, she'd paced her apartment, chewed at her nails, despaired of what to do. Confront Bella herself? Call Reid McCormack for help? Or go home and tell her sisters everything? Maybe talking it through with her sisters would help her decide what to do, and since Bella was her friend, Zoe really did deserve to have a say in the matter.

But no matter what she did where Bella and Zaccaro Fashions were concerned, she found herself having an even harder time figuring out what to do about Nigel.

Oh, how she was dreading that. So many times during the night, she'd considered flying back to New York without a word to him or anyone else at Ashdown Abbey. And in fact she'd started packing her things, because either way, she knew she would be returning home sooner rather than later.

The thought of seeing Nigel again filled her with equal parts excitement and trepidation. Excitement because every time she saw him brought a thrill of delight and desire. Trepidation because she'd been lying to him all along and might now have to come clean, telling him everything.

He would hate her, of course. Hate her, be furious with her, possibly blow up at her before having her dragged from the building like a common criminal. Which was no less than she deserved, she knew.

Her pulse was frantic, beating louder and louder in her ears the closer she got to her desk and the door of Nigel's office. Before leaving her apartment, she'd called Reid McCormack again, this time glad when his secretary put her through and he picked up in person.

He'd been short with her at first, on the verge of reading her the riot act, she suspected. But she'd quickly redirected his anger by filling him in on what she was really doing in Los Angeles and what she'd discovered. They made an appointment for her to bring everything she'd found to his office the following week, where he could look it over and they would decide what steps to take next.

Then she called her sisters. For a change, she'd actually been hoping one of them would answer, but with the time difference between New York and California, she'd gotten only voice mail both at home and on their cells. Instead of the message she'd planned to leave before figuring out who was behind the design thefts, she'd told them where she was and that she'd be home within the next few days.

She hadn't told them *why* she was in Los Angeles or why she'd taken off the way she had, but assured them she was fine and would fill them in when she got back. In fact, she ended her message with *there's a lot we need to talk about*. And, boy, was there ever. She only hoped this entire situation wouldn't end up putting a rift between them.

And then she'd picked up her purse and the letter it had taken her most of the night to compose. The ink of which her sweaty palm was probably smearing into illegibility at that very moment.

Her breathing was coming in shallow bursts, her stomach churning and threatening to revolt with every *boom-kaboom-kaboom* of her aching, pounding heart. But as much as it pained her, as much as she wanted to turn tail and run, this was something she had to do.

Swallowing hard, she laid her purse down on top of her—or rather, the future personal assistant's—desk and turned toward Nigel's office. The letter clutched in her hand was wrinkled almost beyond repair. She'd better do this before it became completely unreadable.

Shaking from head to toe, she reluctantly raised an arm and knocked. Nigel responded immediately, calling in his deep British accent for her to come in. His voice snaked down her spine, warming her and causing a shivery chill all at the same time. Pushing the door open, Lily walked inside, her footsteps as heavy as lead weights.

The minute he spotted her, his face lit up…and Lily's heart sank. He was so handsome. So charming and masculine and self-assured. And lately, he'd begun looking at her like she could come to mean something to him.

He was certainly coming to mean something to her. More than she ever would have thought possible, given the fact that he'd originally come here thinking he might be behind the thefts of her designs.

Now it was breaking her heart to think of leaving him. To have to tell him who she really was and why she'd truly been working for him.

She'd tried to deny it, not even letting the thought fully form itself in her mind, but she'd fallen in love with him. With a man who, in only moments, would come to despise her.

"Lillian," he said, and the sound of her name—even her fake name—on his lips nearly brought tears to her eyes.

Pushing back his chair, he rose to his feet and came around his desk. He reached her in record time, before she could register his movements and attempt to stop him. He gripped her arms, leaning in to kiss her cheek and then her mouth.

Heat suffused her, threatening to fog her brain and draw her far, far away from her determination to come clean and tell Nigel the truth. She couldn't help but kiss him back, but curled her fingers into fists to keep from wrapping them around his shoulders or running them through his hair.

Whether he noticed her reluctance or not, she couldn't tell. He was still smiling when he pulled back, which only made her insides burn hotter with regret.

Nigel reached up to brush a stray curl behind her ear, offering a suggestive, lopsided grin. "Did you come in early for our little game of Naughty Secretary?" he asked. "I can't think of a better way to start the day, and would be happy to sweep away all my work so we can make proper use of the desk."

Her throat grew tight and closed on her next breath. She shook her head and blinked back tears.

At her response, his eyes narrowed, his expression growing serious.

"Lillian," he said again, taking her hand and giving it a reassuring squeeze. "You don't look well. What's wrong?"

Clearing her throat, she tried to find her voice, praying she could say what she needed to say without breaking down completely.

"Can I speak with you?" she began, the words thready and weak.

"Of course."

Still holding her hand, he led her to one of the chairs in front of his desk, guiding her into it before turning the other to face her and taking a seat himself.

"What is it?" he asked, concern clear in the hazel-green depths of his eyes.

Hoping he wouldn't notice that she was shaking, she held the letter out to him.

"This is for you."

While he began to open the envelope and take out the piece of paper folded inside, she rushed ahead, knowing that if she didn't get it all out before he began to react to her letter of resignation, she never would.

"I've been lying to you," she said. "The whole time, I've been here under false pretenses. My real name is Lily Zaccaro, and I'm part-owner of Zaccaro Fashions out in New York. I came to Los Angeles and started working for you because someone stole some of my recent designs and used them to create your California Collection. I probably should have handled things differently. I'm sorry," she hastened to add before pausing only long enough to take a much-needed breath.

"I know you'll hate me for this, and I don't blame you. But I want you to know that I didn't do anything to harm you or Ashdown Abbey. I poked around *only* to find out who might have had access to my personal designs and was also involved in the creation of the California Collection. That's all I did. I didn't come here to spy on your operation or steal company secrets or anything like that, I swear."

Eyes stinging, she blinked back tears. Swallowed past the lump of emotion growing bigger and bigger in the center of her throat.

Where only moments before Nigel's features had been relaxed and soft with pleasure when he met her gaze, they were now stone-cold and harshly drawn with both disappointment and betrayal. He stared at her letter in his hand as though it didn't make sense, and she didn't know if he'd heard a word she'd said…or if he'd heard every one and couldn't bear to look at her because of them.

She sat stock-still, afraid to move, afraid to breathe. Simply waiting and bracing herself for his reaction, however ugly it might be.

And then he raised his head, his eyes locking on hers. What she saw there stabbed her straight through: hurt, confusion, betrayal.

"You're leaving," he said, his tone flat, utterly hollow. "You're not who you proclaimed to be, and now that you've gotten what you came for, you're leaving."

She didn't know which was worse—having to explain her actions or hearing him summarize them so succinctly. Both had her stomach in knots of self-loathing.

All she could do was croak out a remorseful "Yes."

The silence that ensued was almost painful. Like nails scraping down a chalkboard, but with no sound, only the uncomfortable tooth-rattling, grating sensation.

A muscle jumped in his jaw, his mouth a flat slash across the lower half of his face. His gaze drifted away from hers, locking on a point at the far side of the room and refusing to return anywhere near her.

One minute ticked by, and then another, while she searched for something, anything to say. But what more was there? She'd already confessed, told him who she really was and why she'd pretended to be his personal assistant. Whatever else she came up with to fill the heavy weight of dead air would only make matters worse.

So she held her tongue, waiting for the dressing-down she knew was coming and that he had every right to level at her.

Instead, he stood and rounded his desk. Still without looking at her, he took a seat in the wide, comfortable leather chair and placed his hands very calmly on the blotter, palms down.

"You should go," he said finally.

Lily licked her lips, swallowed, wished her heart would slow its erratic pace inside her chest. She opened her mouth to speak, even though she had no idea what to say, but he cut her off.

Gaze drilling into her as he raised his head, his voice trickled through her veins like ice. "You're leaving. Your letter of resignation has been turned in, and I've accepted it. You should go."

It wasn't at all how she'd expected things to go. She'd expected angry words and raised voices. Hurt feelings and terrible accusations. This calm, quiet, resigned response was so much worse. Chilling. Heartbreaking. And so very, very final.

With a sharp nod, she gritted her teeth to keep from making a sound. Especially since she could feel a sob rolling up from her diaphragm.

Pushing to her feet, she turned and walked to the door, relieved when she made it the whole way without incident. Reaching out a shaky hand, she gripped the knob and tipped her head just enough to catch a glimpse of him in her periphery.

"I am sorry, Nigel."

Not waiting for a reply, she slipped out of the room and moved toward the elevators as quickly as possible, hoping she could make it inside before she completely fell apart.

Thirteen

One month later...

Lily stood behind the counter of the Zaccaro Fashions store staring out at the porcelain-white mannequins wearing her designs; the displays of other items, like Juliet's handbags and Zoe's *daZZle* line of shoes; and the handful of customers milling about. A sting of pain made her drop her thumb from her mouth as she realized—not for the first time—that she'd bitten the nail down to the quick. All of her formerly beautiful nails were like that now—short and mangled thanks to her apparent need to work off stress by destroying any chance at a decent manicure.

Clutching her hands together behind her back in an attempt to stop the troublesome habit, she turned her attention to the front of the store. Maybe she should rearrange the window displays again. She'd redone them twelve times in the past four weeks, when normally they changed them only once a month or so.

Her sisters were beginning to think she'd gone off the deep end. She knew this because Zoe had come right out and said, "Lil, you're going off the deep end," just a few days ago when the smoke alarm in their apartment had started shrieking yet again because she'd put something on the stove, then walked away and forgotten what she was doing.

She wished she could claim it was the spark of creative passion distracting her and making her borderline psychotic. What she wouldn't give to have new design ideas filling her head and the need to get them down on paper or fitted onto a dress form keeping her up at night.

But no. Since returning from Los Angeles, she hadn't sketched anything more than pointless, shapeless doodles that had nothing to do with fashion design, and she hadn't sewn a damn thing. She'd tried, but her heart…her heart just wasn't in it.

She was beginning to think it was because her heart was still in Los Angeles with a certain British CEO who probably wished he'd never met her.

Her chest tightened at the thought of Nigel and the expression on his face just before he'd told her to go. That she wasn't welcome in his office, his company or his life any longer.

Well, he hadn't said the last out loud, but it had been implied. And she'd heard him loud and clear.

She'd hurt one person in all of this mess; she was just grateful she hadn't hurt more. Upon her return to New York, she'd spilled her guts to her sisters. Told them everything, from the moment she'd realized her designs had been copied, to her brilliant plan to find the thief on her own, to her ill-fated affair with Nigel. And as much as she hadn't wanted to, she'd broken the news to Zoe that her friend Bella was behind the thefts.

Just as she'd expected, Zoe had been devastated. And angry. And guilty that she'd been the one to bring Bella into their apartment, their studio, and give her access to their work to begin with.

But Lily and Juliet weren't holding anything against Zoe in the same way Juliet and Zoe didn't hold it against Lily that she'd kept such a secret and run off to Los Angeles without giving them a clue as to what she was up to. It wasn't as though she'd known what her friend was capable of.

And after a long, exhausting discussion that had lasted well into the night, all three of them—Zoe included—had agreed to turn the evidence and information Lily had dug up over to Reid McCormack to let him do some further investigating. Juliet had even offered to take it to him personally, which surprised Lily, since she'd expected her sister to be angry with the detective for pretending to look for Lily while actually covering for her. That had taken a bit of explaining on Lily's part, too.

Then, if Reid thought they had a strong enough case—and they all knew cases like this, concerning "creative license" or the theft of ideas, were hard to prove—they would proceed as necessary, even if it meant taking legal action against Bella Landry. As upset as she was, it was still something Lily would hate to have to do.

Thank heaven for small favors, she supposed. Her broken heart would eventually mend, and the guilt she felt over betraying and lying to a man she'd come to care for—a lot—would eventually dissipate. She hoped. But she didn't know what she'd do without the love and support and forgiveness of her family. Especially her sisters, who were also her best friends.

"Lily!"

Lily jumped at the sound of her name being called very loudly in her ear. She blinked, turning to find Zoe standing beside her, looking extremely put out.

Brows drawn down in a frown, hands on hips, she shook

her head. "I swear, you're about as useful as a zipper on a pillbox hat these days."

Then she sighed, her tone softening. Tipping her head, she said, "There's someone over there who'd like to speak with you."

Lily followed her sister's line of sight, her heart stuttering to a halt when she saw Nigel standing by the far wall, studying the shelves that displayed some of Zoe's finest—and most expensive—footwear designs. Seeing him again made her breath catch. She forgot to inhale for so long that her chest burned and her head began to spin with little stars blinking in front of her eyes.

"What are you waiting for?" Zoe hissed.

Lily shook her head, swallowing past a throat gone desert dry. She couldn't move. She was locked in place, even as every bone in her body turned to jelly.

With a sound of disgust, Zoe put a hand in the middle of Lily's back and urged her out from behind the counter, then gave her a small shove in the right direction for good measure.

"Go," she told her in a hushed voice. Then, in typical Zoe fashion, she grumbled, "And don't screw it up this time."

Nigel watched Lily walking toward him from the corner of his eye. He wanted to turn to her, cross the rest of the distance between them, grab her up and never let go. Instead, he remained turned slightly away, fighting to school his features, keep his heart from breaking out of his chest.

Blast it all, he'd missed her. As angry as he'd been at her... as hurt by the fact that she'd lied to him, pretended to be someone she wasn't...he'd still missed seeing her, touching her, hearing her laugh, watching her lips curl into a smile. Every day since she'd left, he'd wished she were back...then cursed himself for being such a weak, pathetic fool, so easily swayed by womanly wiles. Again, since he seemed to

be falling into many of the same pitfalls with Lily as he ha~~
with Caroline.

Yet here he was. He'd flown all the way across the coun
try to see her again. And to get some answers to the ques
tions he'd been too bitter and infuriated to ask before she'~~
walked out of Ashdown Abbey and returned to her real lif~~
in New York.

The question was, could he ask them and wait for her re
sponse without reaching for her and saying to hell with any
thing else?

When she was only a few feet away, he turned to face he~~
fully. The sight of her punched him in the gut. If he'd bee~~
breathing to begin with, the air would have puffed from hi~~
lungs in a whoosh.

Fisting his hands at his sides, he forced himself not to reac~~
Outwardly. She didn't need to know that inside, a team o~~
wild horses was running rampant through his bloodstream

She stopped. An arm's length from him, which didn't bo~~
ster his resolve in the least.

"Nigel," she said on a shaky breath. Then she licked he~~
lips nervously. "I mean, Mr. Statham."

Her tentativeness had a calming effect, letting him kno~~
she was just as unsure of this impromptu meeting as he wa~~

"Nigel is fine," he told her, resisting the urge to shove hi~~
hands into his pockets and rock back on his heels. They wer~~
a bit beyond polite social etiquette, after all. "Is there some
where we can talk? Privately."

Licking her lips again, Lily glanced around. There wa~~
a handful of shoppers in the store and a blonde who bore
strong resemblance to Lily—a sister?—behind the counte~~
staring at them curiously. When she caught Nigel's eye, sh~~
glowered at him. Definitely one of the sisters.

After Lily had confessed her true identity, admitting th~~
she'd lied to him, he'd been furious, determined to find

way to punish her for her deception. So of course he'd hired a private investigator to discover as much personal information about her as possible.

She came from money, but had worked to open this store on her own, without a handout from her parents, who could easily afford it.

She had two sisters—one older, one younger—who were partners in the design business. They'd gotten involved after Lily had graduated from design school, but seemed to be no less talented. The oldest sister, Juliet, designed handbags and other accessories, while the youngest sister, Zoe, did shoes. Extremely sexy, fashionable shoes, most with enough heel and sparkle to be noticed from a mile off.

Lily designed all of the clothing for Zaccaro Fashions—and she did it quite well. If he'd known about her talent before all of this, he might even have offered her a design position at Ashdown Abbey. She certainly would have been an asset to the company.

And something else he'd been forced to admit after he and the private investigator had both done a good deal of research: she was right about her designs being copied at Ashdown Abbey. How it had been allowed to happen was still a bit of a mystery, but he'd found enough—a link between one of Ashdown Abbey's employees and Lily's sister Zoe, as well as a distinct similarity between Lily's natural design aesthetic and Ashdown Abbey's recent California Collection—to feel confident it wasn't simply a matter of coincidence.

With a tip of her head, Lily gestured for him to follow her, then led him to the back of the store and through a doorway marked *Personnel Only*.

He was surprised to see that it was part storage space, part workroom. There were sewing machines, cutting tables, dress forms and supplies set up, but no one was using them at the moment.

The door clicked shut behind them, and Nigel turned to face Lily, who was standing with her back to the closed panel hand clinging to the round brass knob.

Taking a deep breath that raised her chest and drew his attention to her breasts beneath the brightly patterned top he now recognized as one hundred percent her personal creation she said, "Why are you here, Nigel?"

Right to the point. And regaining a bit of her natural confidence, he noticed. Just one of the things he admired about her, and had from the beginning.

"I thought we should talk," he answered honestly. "You ran off so quickly we didn't have a chance to discuss you true reason for being at Ashdown Abbey."

Lily opened her mouth, clearly eager to set him straight but he held up a hand, stopping her.

"I know—my fault entirely. I told you to go, and at tha point, I was too stunned and angry at your confession to hea the whole story. But I've had some time to think and to calm down, and I have some questions that only you can answer."

She considered that for a second, then offered a small nod "All right. I really am sorry for what I did, for…lying to you I'll tell you whatever you want to know."

As simple as that, and suddenly he couldn't think of bloody thing to say. His mind had been spinning with questions for weeks, his body tense with the need for answers Now Lily was standing in front of him, ready to bare her soul and all he really wanted was to close the distance between them, clutch her tight to the wall of his chest, and kiss he until the rest of the world melted away.

Minutes ticked by, the silence almost deafening. He glossy, periwinkle eyes blinked at him, waiting.

Blowing out a breath, he stiffened his spine, telling him self to man up and do what he'd flown all this way to do.

But again, only a single thought filled his head. Not th

desire to kiss her…that was still there, but taking a close backseat to the one question he most wanted an answer to.

"Our time together," he began, forcing the words past a throat gone tight with emotion. "In Florida, and then after we returned to Los Angeles…did it mean anything to you, or was that, too, part of your strategy?"

Seconds passed while she didn't respond, and his heart pounded so hard he feared she could hear it from halfway across the room.

Finally, her lips parted and air sawed from her lungs on a ragged stutter. Eyes glossy with moisture, her voice cracked as she said, "It meant…everything."

Relief washed over him. Relief and…so much more.

"Oh, Nigel." Lily sighed, dropping all semblance of distance—physical or otherwise—and rushing to him. Her fingers wrapped around his forearms, digging through the material of his suit jacket to the muscle beneath.

"I'm so sorry about everything. I was only trying to find out what happened with my designs. I knew they had been stolen, but I didn't know how or by whom, and I knew I would sound crazy if I started tossing out accusations without proof. I just wanted to poke around a little, see what I could find. I *never* meant to lie to you…not really. And I never, *ever* meant to hurt you, I swear."

She shook her head, glancing away for a moment before looking back, the tears on her lashes spilling over to trail down her cheeks. Nigel felt emotion welling up inside his chest as well, and swallowed to hold it back.

"What happened between us…" she continued. "It was never part of the plan, but I'm not sorry. My feelings for you were completely unexpected, and they made everything so much harder, so much worse. But they were very, very real."

Releasing her hold on his arms, Lily stepped back, not sure if her admission had made things better…or worse.

She felt better now that she'd had the chance to tell Nigel the truth, to tell him how much their time together had meant to her. Not because of her "investigation," not because it absolved her of guilt, but because she'd wanted him to know all along that their relationship hadn't been a casual one. Not to her.

He might not share her feelings. For all she knew, she had been beyond casual to him—disposable, even. But she didn't want him to think, even for a minute, that she'd slept with him as a means to an end. That seduction had been just one more way of using him, lying to him.

At the very least, she'd been able to tell him as much and wouldn't have to live the rest of her life with it hanging over her head. Already, her conscience was lighter for having come clean.

Now only her heart was heavy from having him for such a short time, then losing him to her own stupidity.

Taking a deep breath, she braced herself for whatever his reaction might be. Laughter? An angry scoff? An arrogant quirk of his brow when he realized he'd managed to make another of his personal assistants fall madly in love with him?

Not that she could blame him entirely for the last, if that was the case. She wouldn't be surprised if every person who'd ever worked for him had fallen for him. She'd worked for him only a few short weeks and had fallen head over heels.

The good news, she supposed, was that she had the rest of her life to get over him. It promised to be an agonizing forty or fifty years.

But he didn't laugh or scoff or raise an arrogant brow. He simply held her gaze, something dark and intense flashing behind his hazel eyes.

Resisting the urge to squirm, she linked her hands in front of her and said, "I'm sorry. That was probably more than you wanted to hear. And you have more questions."

Another minute ticked by while he stared down at her, making beads of perspiration break out along her hairline.

Finally, he cleared his throat and gave his head a small shake. "I have to say, I'm disappointed."

Her heart sank. She'd bared her soul, confessed all, come close to throwing herself at him and begging him to love her in return. And he was disappointed.

"Did I mention that you were the best personal assistant I've ever had?" he continued, oblivious to the sobs filling her head as every hope, every dream, every might-have-been died a painful death inside of her.

"And now I find out that you're actually a fairly successful fashion designer in your own right, not a personal assistant at all. You know what this means, don't you?" Without waiting for a reply, he murmured, "I have to start over, interviewing for a new assistant."

He sighed. "I suppose it's for the best. The gossip mill tends to run rampant when executives begin dating their employees. It may not be so bad if we're simply so-called rivals in the world of design."

Lily blinked, feeling as though she'd lost time. He wasn't making sense. Or maybe she'd blacked out for a moment and missed a chunk of the conversation that would help her understand what he was saying.

Hoping she wasn't about to make a giant fool of herself, she mumbled, "You don't have to worry about any of that. I won't tell anyone about our involvement. No one ever needs to know what happened."

A single dark brow quirked upward. "Well, someone is bound to figure it out eventually when they see us together."

Lily tipped her head, frowning in confusion. And her confusion only deepened when he smiled at her. A kind, patient smile she would never expect to see on the face of a man who hated her.

"I had a lot of questions in mind when I walked in here," he told her. "More, probably, than you can imagine. But only one question really matters, and you answered it."

He took a step forward, his hand coming up to stroke her cheek. Her lashes fluttered, pleasure rolling through her at even that brief contact. While he spoke, his thumb continued to brush back and forth along her skin, making her want to weep.

"For the record, it meant something to me, too. Our time together. I've never gotten involved with an employee of the company before. Certainly not one of my assistants. But you…" He shook his head, one corner of his mouth tipping up in a grin and desire flickering in his eyes. "You, I just couldn't seem to resist."

Lily didn't know how she managed to remain upright when her whole body felt like one big pile of sand. Laughter— happy, weightless, delighted laughter—bubbled inside of her, building until it couldn't help but spill out.

Smile widening, Nigel leaned down and kissed her, his lips warm and soft and familiar. For long minutes, she clung to him, unable to believe he was really here, kissing her, telling her these things, making her think maybe, just maybe they had a shot.

All too soon, Nigel lifted his head, breaking the kiss, but not letting her go.

"I think I've fallen quite madly in love with you, Lily Ann Zaccaro. And I'd very much like the chance to start over. No secrets, no lies, no ulterior motives. And no mysterious hidden identities, regardless of how adorable you might look in those sexy-librarian glasses of yours," he added, one corner of his mouth twisting with wry humor. "That is, if you're willing."

"Willing?" she squeaked, barely able to believe *he* was willing to give her a second chance after how she'd deceived him. Or that he was so quick to admit he'd fallen in love with her, when she'd been all but certain feelings like those were hers and hers alone.

If it was true, if he was truly in love with her, she was willing to do just about anything to make things work.

He nodded solemnly. "It won't be easy, considering that we're both tied rather strongly to opposite coasts. But thankfully I have access to a corporate jet and am not above abusing the privilege. I also suspect it will require rather a lot of romantic candlelit dinners. Probably a bevy of bold, romantic gestures on my part. You know—flowers, expensive jewelry, blowing off business commitments to spend amorous weekends in exotic locales. And you'll be expected to *ooh* and *ahh* appropriately at each of them until I've won you over completely. Do you think that's something you can handle?"

Lily laughed. *Giggled* might be a better description. She couldn't seem to help herself. "I'll certainly try," she said, striving to match his falsely sober tone of voice.

"I was also thinking we could work together to get to the bottom of how your designs ended up being used at Ashdown Abbey," he said, brows pulling together in a frown as he grew truly serious for a moment. "I've already suspended Bella Landry's employment at the company, but I can't outright fire her without proof that she stole designs from you and applied them to her efforts for us. Especially since she's denying the accusation. We're looking into it, though. We'll turn over every rock and review every slip of paper in the place until we get to the bottom of it, I assure you."

"Thank you," she murmured, touched by his earnestness on her behalf.

"I'm spearheading the investigation myself, but I could use a bit of help from you, since you're the one most familiar with the designs that were stolen and how they were used in our collection. Fair warning, however—it may require spending a lot of hours alone together, many of them running into the wee hours of the night when we may grow tired and feel the need to lie down for a spell."

At the last, he waggled one dark brow and offered her a lopsided grin.

Once again, a chuckle worked its way up from her belly. She'd never expected him to be able to make her laugh so much, especially when it came to something so serious.

"I'll keep that in mind," she replied, her own lips twitching with amusement.

"I also thought you might consider coming home to England with me."

At that, her eyes widened.

"My father has been complaining for months now that I've gone soft, let your American ways dictate how I run the company. I'd like him to meet you, see just how much I've decided to embrace America—and you."

He offered her a wide and wicked grin. "I actually think he'll be quite taken with you. And after he hears what you did in order to protect your company and designs, I'm pretty sure he'll decide you could be a *good* influence on me."

A beat passed while he let her absorb this latest pronouncement.

"What do you say? Willing to give it a go and see if we're as compatible outside of the office as we were as boss and secretary? And if you survive a visit with my parents, perhaps we can discuss making our relationship a little more... permanent."

Ten minutes ago, she'd thought he hated her. Ten minutes before that, she'd been considering joining a convent and devoting herself to a life of silence and chastity because she'd known she could never be truly happy without him.

Now, she was *too* happy not to agree to almost anything. Even meeting his parents, a prospect that she wasn't ashamed to admit scared her half to death.

"I'd say it sounds like you want to use me for some sort of personal gain," she teased after a moment of collecting her thoughts. "But then, I guess I owe you one on that score."

He tugged her closer, until her breasts pressed flat to his chest and his heat seeped through their clothes straight into her skin. "Very true. But only if you love me as much as I love you."

"Oh, I do love you, Nigel. I really, really do," she admitted, the words filling her with emotion and causing them to catch in her chest. "I still can't believe you're here, telling me you feel the same. So I guess my answer is...*yes*." Yes to everything, always, as long as it was with him.

He kissed her again, quick and hard, pulling her against him so tightly, she could barely breathe. Not that she needed air when she was with him.

"Brilliant," he said, sounding slightly choked up himself for a moment before clearing his throat. "Although you should know that I'm not at all opposed to you using me again in the future. Preferably when we're alone and naked. Feel free to use me however you like then."

"Really?" Her gaze narrowed, all kinds of delightfully wicked thoughts spilling through her head.

"Well..." she said, dragging the word out, flattening her palm against the hard planes of his pectoral muscles hidden beneath the thousand-dollar-silk-cotton blend of his suit jacket and dress shirt. "I'm pretty sure my apartment is empty. Zoe is working here at the store, and Juliet is off for the day with her fiancé. We would be completely alone. And if you like...naked."

A devilish glint played over his features, sending a shock of eagerness down Lily's spine.

"I hope this means you're offering to use me again. Slowly and for a very long time."

"I think that can be arranged," she told him in a low voice.

Going on tiptoe, she pressed her lips to the corner of hi
mouth, his jawline, just beneath his ear. "And then you ca
do the same to me."

Wrapping his arms around her waist like a vise, he lifte
her off her feet and started toward the door, kissing her alon
the way.

"The key to a successful relationship is compromise," h
murmured. "And sharing. And mutual sacrifice."

"And being naked together as often as possible."

Teeth flashed wolfishly as he grinned, swooping in fo
another ravishing kiss.

"That would be my very favorite part."

* * * * *

#2227 SHE'S HAVING THE BOSS'S BABY
Kate Carlisle

Ellie Sterling has baby plans involving a visit to an out-of-town sperm bank. But her boss, Aidan Sutherland, needs her right by his side, and he'll do anything—even offer to get her pregnant!—to keep her there.

#2228 A *VERY* EXCLUSIVE ENGAGEMENT
Daughters of Power: The Capital
Andrea Laurence

When Liam Crowe, the new owner of a scandal-racked news channel, fakes an engagement with his sexiest employee to save the network, it isn't long before real sparks fly and real vows are spoken.

#2229 THE TEXAN'S CONTRACT MARRIAGE
Rich, Rugged Ranchers
Sara Orwig

Will Texas trueblood Marek Rangel's vow to never love again stand the test of a paper marriage to gorgeous Camille Avanole, whose adorable baby desperately needs a daddy?

#2230 THE RETURN OF THE SHEIKH
Kristi Gold

Sheikh Zain Mehdi must shed his bad-boy reputation. Enter political consultant Madison Foster. But Zain doesn't want her advice on how to be a good king—he wants *her*....

#2231 TEMPORARILY HIS PRINCESS
Married by Royal Decree
Olivia Gates

Prince Vincenzo D'Agostino will make Glory Monaghan—the woman who once betrayed him—his temporary princess, get her out of his system, then discard her again as she deserves. Or will he?

#2232 STRADDLING THE LINE
The Bolton Brothers
Sarah M. Anderson

Falling for a wealthy outsider could destroy everything Josey White Plume has worked for, unless she can find a way to straddle the line between his world and hers.

You can find more information on upcoming Harlequin® titles, free excerpts and more at www.Harlequin.com.

HDCNM0413

Juliet Zaccaro stared down at the little plastic wand in he
hand, clutched between shaky, white-knuckled fingers.

It was one of those kits that promised one hundred per
cent accuracy. And that was definitely a giant blue plus sign
glaring back at her like a flashing Broadway marquee.

She was pregnant.

Knees growing weak, she sank onto the closed toilet lid
in a cloud of gauzy white crepe and tulle.

It was her wedding day. Here she was in the cramped
bathroom at the rear of the church where she'd been getting
ready, and she was very unexpectedly, this-is-not-good
news pregnant.

She had no idea what to do about it. She couldn't very
well walk down the aisle and start a new life with a man
who most likely wasn't—who was she kidding?—*definitely*
wasn't the father of her child.

A tap on the bathroom door startled her out of her spiral
ing thoughts. She heard her sister's muffled voice.

"Juliet. We're ready for you, sweetie," Lily said.

"I'll be right there."

"Okay. We'll be waiting in the vestibule."

She wiped away any lingering trace of unshed tears and made sure her eyeliner and mascara were still intact. Then she fluffed out the diaphanous folds of her gown—designed by Lily—and dropped the test stick into the wicker waste-basket beside the sink.

She left the bathroom, crossed the outer room and stepped into the hallway. The whispers of her sisters and father reached her from where they were waiting only a few yards away.

Turn left and she would be at the start of the aisle, step-ping her way into a new life to the strains of "The Wedding March."

Turn right toward one of the church's side doors and she could escape.

Left or right? Go through with the wedding, or throw it all away and dive headfirst into the great unknown?

Time seemed to slow as her ears filled with the hollow, echoing sound of ocean waves. And then she did the only thing she could do. She turned right…

…and ran.

Don't miss

PROJECT: RUNAWAY BRIDE
by USA TODAY *bestselling author Heidi Betts.*

Available in January 2014 from Harlequin® Desire
wherever books are sold.